BLOOD SCENT

A JUNKYARD DRUID URBAN FANTASY NOVELLA

M.D. MASSEY

MODERN DIGITAL PUBLISHING

1

I was at a bar, some random dive I'd stumbled into with bad intentions. I didn't necessarily have bad intentions toward anyone else. They were for myself, mostly. I'd come here to drown my sorrows, to sit at the bar and get shit-faced drunk without hurting anyone or anything but my liver and a few brain cells.

I was already halfway to oblivion, drinking some happy hour concoction named after a body part likely to require routine waxing. It was a buck a drink and it contained alcohol, and that's all I cared about. I was getting numb and close to not caring about a damned thing, and that was the only item on my agenda for the evening.

That's when I noticed the guy at the end of the bar slipping something in his date's drink. I'd been watching him since I'd arrived, mostly out of habit more than a desire to watch my back. Habit had also called for me to sit in the farthest corner of the room—where I had a clear view of the front entrance, restrooms, and every other patron in the bar.

It's not like I cared if anyone snuck up on me. Heck, they were welcome to try. The average human might even get lucky on a night like tonight... and one of the fae or another supernatural creature had even better chances. I wasn't worried. Say they got a lucky shot in, even a killing blow.

That'd just bring *him* out... and that wouldn't be good for anyone.

So, I stuck to my usual habits—not out of self-preservation, but to keep everyone else around me safe.

All I'd wanted was a quiet night in a dive bar, and a few hours of memory loss. Preferably without a single supernatural denizen of the city in sight. That's why I was pissed when I saw the guy roofie his date. It would've pissed me off in any case, but there was something odd about how he did it. His hands moved too fast for the normal eye to see.

My senses tingled. As a born champion, I was genetically gifted—or cursed—with enhanced strength, speed, reflexes, sight, smell, and hearing. Not superhumanly gifted, but certainly a cut above the average human. A black swan, you could say.

While helpful in some situations, it also made me a magnet for supernatural activity. Whether it was something in my genes that drew them to me or something in that same genetic makeup that made me seek them out, I had no idea. But every born champion was destined or doomed to run into creatures that normal people had no idea existed.

Most of us failed to survive our first brush with the world beneath.

And if you survived?

Usually you ended up like me. A monster hunter. *Former* monster hunter, in my case. Someone who'd made a career of dealing with the other side, and who likely regretted surviving that first deadly encounter.

Because no good ever came out of dealing with the other side. Not as an enemy, and certainly not as an ally. Someone always ended up hurt, or dead, or worse. Maybe a loved one, maybe a friend, maybe an innocent who just got caught up in their predatory games.

For me it had been my hunting partner and girlfriend, Jesse, who'd paid the ultimate price. That was why I had decided to tie one on tonight. At least until this prick fucked up my plans.

As for this girl, I could see why he was targeting her. She stood maybe five-foot-five—five-nine in those heels she wore—and when he cracked a joke, her smile lit up like Christmas at the Rockefeller Center. She was fit and had curves in all the right places—with dark-brown hair that fell in waves around her shoulders, and sea-foam eyes that sparkled when she smiled. But she was lower-middle class all the way, on the bottom rung of the life ladder in corporate America. Probably struggling to make ends meet—maybe with a kid or two at home, and a deadbeat ex who never paid his child support on time—and a month behind on her car payment.

The type of vulnerable individual who was just dying for someone, *anyone* to rescue them from a life that was just one miserable slog after the next, with no hope in sight. I knew the type. She could've been my mom before her art career had taken off, in those years after my dad had passed on. Lonely, desperate, and hurting.

The perfect target for a vampire.

Normally, if I saw something like that happen human to human, I'd tip off the bartender or security and let them handle it. But, in this case, the club staff simply weren't equipped to handle the creep in question. That meant I'd have to handle it myself.

"Fuck." I downed the rest of my incredibly nasty drink, trying to ignore the turpentine taste that meant the club refilled their bottles with swill. I dropped a fiver on the bar, nodding to the barkeep as I stood. "One more, if you don't mind. And keep the change."

She did as I asked. I grabbed the drink, swerving slightly as I made my way to the end of the bar. Most of it was intentional... some not so much. Just as I drew even with the couple, I pretend-stumbled and spilled my drink all over the guy's shirt.

He stood immediately, giving me a look that said he'd have killed me if the girl wasn't watching. He was tall, blonde, and handsome—unnaturally so. Well-dressed, in the manner that only people with real money could pull off. I checked him out as I swayed in place, feigning surprise at my faux pas. Thousand-dollar Buschemi shoes, Rolex Oyster, designer jeans, polo shirt, and Ralph Lauren sports coat. *A vamp, for sure.* Probably had gotten turned in the late eighties, I figured. Vamps often made that mistake—sticking with the same manner of dress that had been popular at the time of their demise and rebirth.

I decided to call him Crockett.

He busied himself with wiping off his shirt and pants with napkins from the bar, as the woman hid a smile behind her hand. I could sense his anger, even though he was trying to play it off so he didn't lose his prey.

Whatever the woman was drinking, it was clear and bubbly. I decided to kill two birds with one stone.

"Oh, I am shlow sorry," I slurred, weaving in place as I gestured at my handiwork. "That looks expenshive—here, I know what will take that stain right out."

I grabbed her drink from the bar—the one that had been roofied—and tossed it in his face.

"Shit, I am shush a klutz. Here, let me help you, buddy." I leaned in and grabbed the hem of my t-shirt, acting like I was going to use it to wipe his face.

The man backed up and raised his hands defensively. "It's alright, I have it in hand." He looked at his date. "Char-

Blood Scent5

lene, be a dear and wait for me here, will you? I'm just going to go to the men's room and see if I can dry myself off."

Something was up with his shirt, because the drink I'd spilled on him was barely noticeable. I leaned toward him with a gravity-defying motion that involved my whole body, nearly stumbling into him so I could get a closer look.

"Are you sure I can't help wif zat?"

"Positive," he hissed, then turned on his heel and stomped off to the bathroom.

I watched him enter the facilities, then straightened up and turned to the woman. "Miss, I hate to tell you this, but I saw that guy slip a roofie in your drink."

Her eyes widened. "What? Raffy would never do that. I mean, he's such a gentleman..." I grabbed hold of her as she nearly fell off the barstool and reeled like a drunk. "Oh, my. I do feel a bit woozy."

That meant he'd drugged her already. Probably had done it again when the first dose hadn't taken effect quickly enough. *Damn.*

"We need to call you a cab and get you out of here, now." I called the bartender over. "She's been drugged, and she needs a cab," I told her. Charlene staggered again. "Scratch that, make it an ambulance."

The bartender nodded as she reached for the phone. "Should I call the bouncer?"

I shook my head. "No, this guy's dangerous. I'll handle it."

She looked me over and smirked. "You look a little young to be a cop. You ex-military?"

"Something like that." She looked unconvinced. "I'm a bail enforcement officer, and the guy is a fugitive, alright?"

I turned and looked her in the eye as I said it, willing her to believe my story. Whether she did or not, I couldn't tell. I took a

deep breath and squared my shoulders as I monitored the bathroom entrance.

"If you hear a lot of commotion after I go in there, evacuate
the bar."

"Seriously? I can't do that. It's happy hour. My boss would
kill me."

"Just trust me, okay? And get her out of here, now."

"Okay already. Consider it done."

I listened for a moment as she dialed 911, then I headed for
the men's bathroom.

2

I pulled a silver-plated dagger from my Craneskin Bag with my left hand, and hefted a Glock loaded with silver-tipped bullets in my right. I placed the butt of the knife on the door, pausing before I pushed it open to enter the restroom. There was a short entryway, then the room opened to the right.

I sliced the pie, inching slowly around the corner—the same way cops and spec ops soldiers cleared rooms. I was careful not to flag my presence with the muzzle of the pistol. The idea was to get the jump on this vamp, not to *get* jumped.

Nothing. I ducked down and looked under the stalls. *Strike two.* I kicked open the stall doors, one at a time, gun and dagger at the ready.

Strike three. Damn.

I looked up and spotted an open window, high along the wall above the sinks. I debated letting the vamp go, then decided that as long as "Raffy" was out there, he was a danger to Charlene and other women. I needed to take him out before he tracked her down and finished whatever he'd intended to do to her.

And I doubted he'd wanted to surprise her with a mani-pedi.

I secreted the knife inside my jacket and tucked the pistol in my waistband at the small of my back. It was a crappy way of carrying a loaded pistol, but I just needed to hide it until I left the bar. The paramedics arrived as I walked out of the bathrooms. Charlene was sitting at a booth near the front, and the bartender was holding her up so she didn't slip to the floor.

I waited until the paramedics began treating her, then used the distraction to slip out the door. I hated leaving the girl like that, but in my line of work—or, rather, my former line of work —it paid to be inconspicuous and forgettable. So, the fewer questions the staff and medics asked me, the better.

Outside the bar, I looked left and right to get my bearings. The bathroom was in the back of the club, but these buildings were built right next to each other with shared walls. I jogged around the block to the alley, sobering up as the reality of what I might be facing caught up to me.

Thanks to my *other* side, which always kicked in when I was near death, I wasn't really in danger. Back when I'd first lost Jesse, I'd tried a dozen different ways to end my misery. None of them had worked. Then again, I hadn't tried beheading myself or ripping my own throat out—or yanking my heart out of my chest. A vampire of sufficient age might be capable of any of those things, and I had no idea if my other form could heal from such a mortal wound.

Death by vampire. Maybe... I shook my head and cleared the thought from my mind. Dr. Larsen, my therapist, had instructed me to avoid entertaining such thoughts. It was a pointless exercise anyway, so I mostly did as she asked.

As I rounded the corner to the alley, it took me a second to catch my breath. Getting winded from such a short run was embarrassing, considering what I'd once been. I'd been taught how to hunt and kill fae creatures and monsters by someone who'd been doing it for thousands of years. If he saw me like this, he'd never let me live it down. But when you were dealing with chronic depression, it wasn't like you had the desire to stay in shape.

But tonight—for the first time in quite a while—I felt all those old, familiar sensations: an elevated pulse, a tingling up my spine, and a heightened awareness of sound and movement. All the little things that make an adrenaline-junkie-slash-hunter go back for more, job after job and night after night. I had to admit, I was liking it—against my better judgment.

But I still had a vampire to deal with. I pulled the knife and gun. I cast a simple cantrip to enhance my vision, so I could see past the pool of light I currently stood in. City sounds and smells played in the night air around me: traffic from the other side of the buildings on the main drag, garbage and vomit from the trash receptacle nearby, and the sound of my blood rushing in my ears.

Oh yeah, I need this. Probably more than I cared to admit.

I stalked into the alley, my every sense on full alert. The cantrip began to kick in, and where there had been darkness a moment before, I began to make out vague shapes in hues of gray. Bags of garbage, dumpsters, empty beverage crates—that sort of thing. But no sign of my vampire.

Then, I sensed something above me. I rolled out of the way, just as "Raffy" pounced on the spot where I'd been standing. I came up in a kneeling position, firing off two shots as he pivoted and sped back into the darkness above.

Oh yeah, he's a full-fledged vamp, I thought. I hadn't really been sure, since some Renfields could exhibit vampire-like abilities, depending on how recently they'd been fed by their masters. Humans sometimes worked out symbiotic relationships with vamps, trading blood for blood. A smart master vamp would get several humans hooked on his heme, giving him a steady supply of food and day walkers to do his bidding.

But what they didn't usually tell humans was that eventually, the vamp blood would turn them undead. And not sparkly-pretty vampire undead, either. No, at some point they'd either go ghoul or turn into a revenant—a sort of weaker, decomposing vampire. A zompire, if you will. Revs were dangerous, more so than ghouls; but that's not what this guy was.

Nope, by the way he'd moved, he was a full-fledged Count Chocula. And I had no idea where he was at the moment. I decided to try to draw him out.

"The girl is long gone by now. I had the barkeep call for an ambulance. You may as well give up and go home. Or, you could come out into the light and face me. Your choice."

There was no reason to tip the vamp off that I could see in the dark. Right now, he was hiding—probably on the roof of a nearby building. But if he didn't know I could see him, I'd hopefully be able to spot him as he snuck about in the shadows.

A voice replied from everywhere and nowhere. "Yes, hunter, I am aware. I overheard your conversation after I retired to the bathroom. You see, I could tell you weren't that inebriated. A man of your size couldn't possibly be that drunk. I kept track of what you'd had to drink the whole time."

Oh, this guy was a real peach. Not all vamps were so gifted. Most just came with your garden variety strength and speed. Others might luck out, and win the vyrus lottery. Vyrus was a purposeful misspelling, a combination of "vampyre" and "virus." It was what gave vamps their powers. A lucky vamp, or one who was a few centuries old, they might get an extra power... the ability to fly, or turn invisible, or transform into another creature. But that was rare.

This guy could throw his voice. It might have been a learned skill, but I doubted it. That indicated age or power—or both. I needed to be on my guard.

"So, you made me for a hunter. Whoop-dee-doo. That means

you knew I'd follow you out here, too. Living on the edge, eh Raffy?"

The voice echoed from the other end of the alley. "I'd hoped you'd follow. Hunter blood is just as sweet as that of an innocent. Although, Charlene could hardly be considered pristine. She's a bit used up for her age—but she would have been worth the trouble just the same."

I waited several seconds, every sense attuned to the night. He'd stopped talking, which meant he was about to strike.

His whisper filled my ear. "But I suppose you'll have to do."

I stabbed back in an underhanded swing with the knife, just as he pinned my upper arms to the sides of my body. That negated much of the power in the motion, but I still connected with something and felt the knife sink into flesh. The vamp screamed in my ear—a blood-curdling sound that emptied his lungs. His fetid breath smelled of clotted blood and vyrus.

I stabbed a second and third time. He released one of my arms so he could strike me, or perhaps to take away the knife. Rather than spinning away like any rational human would, I went limp and dropped, narrowly missing a swipe from his hand that might very well have taken my head off. He was still hanging onto me with his other hand, but by turning toward him as I collapsed, I was able to bring the gun to bear.

I planted the barrel in his stomach and emptied four rounds into him. Normally on a hunting job, I'd load my magazines with specialty ammo suited for the occasion. But whenever I had no idea what I might be facing, I alternated ammo types as I loaded my mags.

Cold-iron pellets embedded in hollow points. Silver-tipped rounds. Rowan wood bullets that were only accurate at close range, but played hell when they hit certain creatures. And tracer rounds, because vamps and some other types of undead were susceptible to fire.

I'd hit him with all four.

I heard a grunt escape his lips, then the vamp tossed me like a ragdoll across the alleyway. I collided with a wall, struck my head against a metal gutter drain, and fell to the pavement below.

Shaking it off, I rolled over and pointed the gun toward where I'd been standing just moments before. But the vamp was gone. And I had a splitting headache.

"Damn it," I cursed. "I need another drink."

3

I stormed into Luther's place with a bad attitude and violence on my mind. I walked up to the coffee bar, shouldering an office jockey with a cheap haircut and expensive suit out of the way.

"Hey!" he exclaimed. I glanced over my shoulder and locked eyes with him, briefly. He must've seen murder there, because he decided to grab a seat and wait his turn.

Luther was behind the bar, arms crossed. He eyed me with amused interest. Like most higher vamps, he was unnaturally good-looking, self-assured, and not at all concerned at my entrance. That just pissed me off.

I mean, sure—walking into a higher vampire's place of work and calling him out in front of all and sundry was suicide. Especially when the vamp in question headed up the local vampire population, and a good number of his people worked in said establishment.

But then again, I hadn't been very concerned with my own safety lately.

I slammed the lab report down on the counter. "I thought

you and your brood were supposed to be different," I growled. My voice was icy-calm but filled with venom, and I scowled as I stared at him across the counter. "I'm here to tell you that you aren't going to do this shit in my town. Not while I'm around."

Out of the corner of my eye, I saw two patrons and a barista tense. *Luther's bodyguards*, I thought. *Missed the one by the door. I must be slipping.*

His eyes narrowed, but the amused smile never left his face. "If it's death you're looking for, that can be arranged," he whispered, too low for mundane ears to hear. He spoke with an accent that was one part flamboyant gay and two parts New Orleans old money. "But before you act rashly, you might consider whether this all might be a terrible misunderstanding."

"Read the report," I seethed. "There's no misunderstanding at all."

I'd stolen the lab report from Charlene's chart the night before, when I'd snuck into the hospital to check on her. It had cost me my last twenty bucks to get the bartender to tell me where they'd transported her, but the proof and peace of mind had been worth it. I pushed the sheet of paper across the bar at Luther, an accusation in black and white.

He ignored the gesture, and instead maintained eye contact with me. "I already did, the moment you set it down. Now, before you embarrass yourself further—and do something you'll regret—let's retire to my office so we can discuss this matter in a more civil and less public fashion."

I breathed heavily. My body vibrated with barely restrained anger, balanced on the edge of violent action. I watched him carefully for a few seconds, looking for just a hint of guile or deception. I wanted any excuse to fall off the precipice into the cauldron of bloodlust that constantly roiled inside me of late.

I saw nothing in him but sincerity. Slightly disappointed, I took a deep breath, let it out, and nodded.

"This way, please," he said as he took the bar towel from his shoulder and laid it neatly on the counter. He looked at a barista who had been cleaning tables while pointedly ignoring our conversation. "Orlando, see to our customers. And please, get the man in the Armani with the hairpiece a free coffee, would you?"

"Hey!" the man protested again, touching his hair self-consciously.

"It is a lovely suit, sir." The vampire stared at him with the same smile he'd used on me, but his eyes held something more —something primal, and not altogether friendly.

I sensed a slight push of magic from Luther, then the man nodded, his expression vacant. "A latte will be fine."

So he wasn't just your average vamp. Good to know.

Luther inclined his head at Orlando, who was already heading for the espresso machine. The lackey gave me a look as he passed that said I'd better not try anything. I ignored him, keeping my eyes on Luther. The old vampire smoothly sashayed from behind the counter, gliding with a dancer's grace and a runway model's flair in tight white pants, a dark silk shirt, and two-tone Corthay shoes that cost more than I made in a season.

I might not have been able to afford that kind of style, but I knew it when I saw it.

We entered a room marked "Employees Only," and Luther took a seat in a rather mundane office chair behind an equally boring desk. The office looked like any other, with stacks of invoices, a computer humming quietly in the background, and coffee stains on the desk calendar. I had taken Luther for a neat freak, and suspected this was all for show. Normal business owners were rarely neat and tidy; my uncle Ed was a testament to that fact.

"Please, sit," Luther said as he gestured toward a metal and vinyl chair that sat in front of the desk. I obeyed, clutching the lab report tightly in my hand. He sat back in his chair and regarded me with his eyebrow slightly raised. I decided to let him speak first.

"Generally speaking, I wouldn't normally allow someone to barge into my place in such a rude and unsettling manner." He steepled his fingers and tapped them together slowly as he spoke. "However, I believe you're operating under a grave misunderstanding, so I'm willing to give you a pass."

"You're saying it wasn't one of your people I caught slipping a roofie to some unsuspecting human woman last night?"

He pursed his lips as his eyes narrowed. "I can assure you, it was not. Are you certain it was a vampire?"

"As certain as I can be, without letting it take a chunk out of my neck. Sure moved like one, and smelled of blood and vyrus. And when I shot it with silver, wood, and fire, it seemed to have the desired effect."

He closed his eyes. "I'd prefer that you didn't hunt my kind without asking me first. We have our own methods of dealing with such things in the coven." His eyes snapped back open and zeroed in on me in a dead, unblinking stare that sent a chill down my spine. "But alas, in this case, I believe the situation calls for outside help."

He pulled a file folder from a nearby cabinet and laid it open in front of me. It held newspaper clippings, dated over the past several months. The headlines told a familiar tale, one that I'd seen played out in towns and cities across Texas during my brief yet illustrious career as a hunter.

SUSPECT SOUGHT IN GRUESOME KILLING; VICTIM'S IDENTITY UNKNOWN

32-YEAR-OLD FEMALE FOUND DEAD IN S. AUSTIN HOME, FOUL PLAY SUSPECTED

POLICE DECLARE WOMAN'S DEATH A HOMICIDE

AUSTIN POLICE ASK FOR TIPS IN WEEKEND HOMICIDE CASE

Roughly one killing, every few weeks. I stared at the clippings and headlines, wondering how I'd missed the pattern. I'd been out of the loop for too long, and let one slip by me. Granted, I'd sworn off hunting for good. But if there was a supernatural serial killer in Austin, someone needed to do something about it. Maybe not me, but *someone*.

"How long has this been going on?"

He blinked—once, twice—then stared at the newspaper clippings and sighed. Not for the first time, I realized he was good at blending in. Vampires didn't sigh or blink; not involuntarily, anyway.

"Several months now."

"And you swear he's not one of yours?" I was fairly certain Raffy wasn't, just based on the fact that Luther was connecting a whole lot of murders for me. If it was one of his, he damned sure wouldn't be telling a hunter about it.

He shook his head. "No, of course not. We aren't like the New Orleans coven. Savages, one and all." He shuddered, which I knew was pure theatrics. Still, I liked him for it despite myself.

"No, my people only feed on the willing—and their donors are well-compensated for the services they provide. We are very happy to live among the humans of this city, blending in and enjoying a relatively peaceful existence. To be hunted, or to start a war with the Circle, is the last thing we want. And besides that, I'd kill any of mine who broke my edict against killing humans."

The Cold Iron Circle was a private and powerful organization that consisted of human mages and hunters. They hated monsters and fae both, and had appointed themselves protectors of humanity against all supernatural threats. I was quite certain they'd use any excuse to run Luther and his coven out of town.

"Then you know what I'm going to ask next."

"Why haven't I done anything about these killings?" He adjusted the cuffs on his shirt before answering. "Because I can't catch the bastard. He's too damned smart—knows what I'm going to do before I even know myself. And, he's bringing a ton of heat down on us from the Circle. The last thing I want is for one of my people to be caught at the scene of one of these murders. It's all Gunnarson would need to declare open season on my kind."

I had a feeling he was about to ask me to do something I didn't want to do. I sat and stared at him, trying to maintain a poker face. It was rude, but I had to hide what I was feeling. Indifference seemed to be the best method.

He waited for a response, and when I gave him nothing, he nodded and continued. "I suppose it's your turn to guess my next question."

I closed my eyes for a moment and let out a soft sigh. "I gave that part of my life up. Put it past me, so I could move on."

"Hmmm." He rubbed his palms together. I noticed that his skin looked buttercream soft, although his flesh was likely hard as granite. Vampire physiology was weird that way. "Just out of curiosity, what would your fee be for something like this? You know, just in case I find another freelancer who can get the job done."

I shook my head. "You won't. Most every hunter worth their salt ends up working for the Circle. Job security, medical, dental. Can't blame them, really."

"But if I did, how much would it cost me?"

I hitched my shoulders slightly. "Five hundred a day, plus expenses for a normal vamp. But I have a feeling this one is old. That'd push my fee to seven hundred fifty a day plus."

"I'll double it."

"Luther, I—"

"Fine, I'll triple it then." I looked down and covered my eyes. The offer was tempting. "Colin, someone has to deal with this... *monster* before he kills again. My hands are tied—but you? Well, you're the perfect answer to this problem."

"I already have a job, Luther." I came to my feet and extended my hand. "Thanks for not taking my head off when I stormed into your place."

He stood and shook my hand. I'd been right; his flesh was hard and cool. "Thanks for listening to reason. Damned shame I can't hire you, though. The coven could really use your assistance."

"Yeah, sorry I can't help you." I turned toward the door, but Luther's voice stopped me in mid-stride.

"And, Colin? I hope I'm not being too forward, but I am aware of your recent loss. I realize this must be a very difficult time for you, and I want you to know that I don't think less of you for refusing to help."

I nodded once and walked out the door.

THAT NIGHT ON THE NEWS, they announced that Charlene Thomas, thirty-four years of age, mother of two, had been murdered in her south-side apartment. Her children had been asleep in the next room when it happened. The news report indicated her oldest had found her. The girl was just seven years old.

I called Luther's cafe. Someone picked up on the other end, although all I heard was silence.

"I'll take the case."

I hung up before anyone could respond. Then I laid back in bed, staring at the ceiling for hours. The more I thought about whether I was making the right choice, the more muddled my thoughts became. Finally, I decided that the *right* choice would have been chasing that motherfucker down and cleaving his head from his shoulders when I'd had the chance. I said a prayer for Charlene's kids, then turned the light off and fell into a restless sleep.

4

I had a serious problem. I'd taken the job and come to grips with my decision, so that moral dilemma had been mostly solved. And as far as the money went, I saw no ethical quandary in getting paid to end Raffy's miserable existence. No, my current issues stemmed from other, more practical and immediate concerns.

Namely, I was in piss-poor shape for hunting vampires. Especially old and powerful fangers who had a grudge against me, like this one probably did. Most vamps healed quickly, so long as they had an ample supply of blood. But healing after getting stabbed and shot with silver, then bullet-staked and burned? Well... that wasn't going to be high on any bloodsucker's list of fun ways to spend an evening.

Chances were good that he'd tracked down and killed Charlene as a sort of "fuck you" message to me. I was still kicking myself over that one. The circumstances surrounding my return to hunting sucked—but the fact was, I had a fire in my belly that I hadn't felt in a very long time.

Only problem was, I'd gone soft during my absence from the game. And that would be a liability, one I needed to address immediately. The good news was, it wouldn't take much time to get back in shape. Being a genetic anomaly, it'd only take a week or two to get me back up to snuff. Problem was, I needed to start tracking this vamp down now. That meant I'd have to get back in shape while I worked the job. It meant I'd also need backup—in case I got in too deep, too soon.

One thing at a time, though.

At least I wasn't worried about dying. What did worry me was getting nearly dead and unleashing that other part of me. The cursed side.

I could not let that happen, under any circumstances. So, I needed to get my ass squared away A-S-A-fucking-P, to ensure that I wouldn't visit widespread death and mass destruction on my city.

Normally I'd go to my mentor, Finnegas. He was an older-than-dirt druid, maybe the last of his kind, and he knew more about killing fae and other creatures than anyone else I'd ever known. He'd trained me and my late girlfriend, Jesse, and had shown us how to hunt and kill everything from alps to wights, to barghests and *weisse frauen*.

But since Jesse's passing, he'd become a drunk and an addict —and he was the last person I wanted to go to now for help in knocking the rust off. So, I did the next best thing; I called his secretary, Maureen. She was old and half-fae—maybe not as old as Finnegas, but old enough to have helped the old man train a number of hunters over the years. She'd been one of our tutors, back when we'd been learning the ropes.

And, she could fight. You'd never know it by looking at her— a tall, flame-haired knockout whose presence had sent my teenage hormones raging on more than one occasion. But she was no shrinking violet. Maureen was skilled in all manner of classical weaponry, and had stood in as our blade craft coach when Finnegas was otherwise engaged.

More importantly, being half-fae, she was physically gifted and possessed certain athletic qualities similar to those of a vampire. Superhuman speed, stamina, reflexes, and so on. Plus, Maureen was good people—one of the few fae I trusted. I dialed the number for Eire Imports, the business Finnegas had used as a cover for our hunting activities. I half-expected there to be no answer.

"Colin, what a pleasant surprise. Is Finn in trouble?"

I smiled at the sound of her voice. While I'd gotten over my crush on Maureen some years past, she was still one of my favorite people. "Hi, Maureen. No, there's nothing going on with the old man."

I listened to the sound of her breathing for the span of a few heartbeats. "I take it he's still off the wagon, then?"

"I think the wagon has left the outpost for good, Maureen. Sorry."

"Well, I've known him for much longer than you've been on this earth. I've seen him come back from worse. Relative immortality has a way of either breaking a person or making them incredibly resilient. Don't count him out yet."

I chose to remain silent. Sometimes it was better to not say anything at all.

"You obviously didn't call to talk about the Seer. Tell me, to what do I owe the pleasure of this conversation?"

"I need your help, Maureen."

"How so?"

I cleared my throat, stalling. After a pause, I finally just spit it out. "I've... taken on a hunting contract."

"Ah, I see. Must be serious, for you to take up arms again and deal with the world beneath." I heard a dull thrumming in the background as she considered what I'd told her. Maureen had always been a fidgeter. "What do you need? Weapons? A support team? I've frozen all of Finn's assets, but I can get to some funds if necessary."

"Not right now. What I actually need is someone to whip me back into shape, and fast."

"And I'm the first person you thought of? Really?"

"Oh, come on, Maureen. Like you didn't have a hand in transforming two kids into stone killers." My voice sounded bitter as I said it, and I regretted it. I blamed Finnegas for Jesse's death, and in that moment I realized that I also felt some anger toward Maureen as well.

She sniffed disdainfully. "And I was branded a traitor to my own kind, for the role I played in teaching you two how to survive. I'd remind you to show a bit of gratitude, or at least some respect for what I gave up for you."

After word had gotten out that she had assisted Finn in producing a team of druid-trained hunters, Maureen had been marked as somewhat of an outcast among local fae society. Still, I got the impression that she'd been at odds with her own kind long before Jesse and I had arrived on the scene. I figured it was because she wasn't entirely fae—or perhaps something else had turned her against the People of the Mounds. Whatever it was, it had made her bitter enemies with certain of her kind.

I kept those thoughts to myself. I needed her on my side, because there simply wasn't anyone else I could turn to who had her skills. At least, no one I could trust.

"It's no secret that I wish I'd never met Finnegas, or that I'd never learned of the world beneath. But I do appreciate what you did for us, Maureen, and I am—what I mean to say is, I remember it well." I took my time after that near-stumble. One had to be careful not to thank the fae. "I know you helped us, the best way you knew how. And now, I need that help again."

She snorted softly. "You have been slipping, to nearly indebt yourself to one of my kind in casual conversation." More thrumming echoed in the background. "I'll expect you at the warehouse in two hours. Be ready to sweat."

The line went dead before I could respond. Typical Maureen. She was sweet as molasses until it came time to get things done. Then, she was all business.

The warehouse she referred to was the storage area behind Eire Imports, in my hometown a couple of hours away. I'd left there and come to Austin to put those sad memories behind me. And, to put some distance between me and my girlfriend's ghost.

Now, it looked like I'd be revisiting old memories—and possibly stirring up spirits that were better left alone. I didn't relish the thought of potentially disturbing Jesse's rest. But even the slightest hope that I might hear from her again made my heart skip a beat.

I looked at her photo, on the shelf next to my door. "Shit, Colin, get it together. It's long past time to move on."

I took a deep breath, steeling myself for what was to come. Then, I busied myself with gathering my gear, trying to put the past out of my mind.

5

I 'd borrowed a junker from Ed for the trip, telling him I wanted to go see Mom. My Vespa just wasn't made for making that haul up IH-35, the deathtrap that it was. The highway, mind you—not the scooter.

I'd probably stop in to see Mom, although I didn't intend to stay over. The last place Jesse had haunted me had been at my mom's house. While I suspected that she was following me around full-time now, anything that triggered a powerful emotional response toward her might cause her to make contact.

Unfortunately, the more she exerted her presence in our world, the more "life energy" she used. And if she used too much before she moved on to the after-life? No more Jesse.

So, I tried to avoid triggering those memories as much as possible. Which meant meeting Maureen at the warehouse was probably a bad idea. Hopefully, she didn't plan to train there. If so, I'd have to suggest an alternative.

Another reason to keep my visit with Mom short and sweet was that I needed to get back to Austin to start looking for Raffy. I wouldn't confront him until I was absolutely ready, but I could at least start tracking him down. And, hopefully, keep him from killing anyone else.

During the drive, I spent time reflecting on my initial encounter with the vamp. I soon reached the conclusion that I had been damned lucky to survive. "Raffy"—which I assumed was short for Rafael—wasn't your run-of-the-mill vamp, not by a long shot. I hoped that a few days of training with Maureen would be enough.

I drove to the warehouse with butterflies in my stomach. The old place held a ton of memories for me—mostly good, but always associated with that one fateful night. It was in what had been an industrial section of the city, not far from the recently revitalized downtown area around the courthouse square.

The building was boarded up, and the parking lot was strewn with trash and debris. It stood out as an eyesore among the transitioning neighborhoods and buildings surrounding downtown. While the neighboring buildings were slowly being converted into restaurants, boutiques, and apartment lofts and studios for up and coming professionals, Eire Imports was falling into disrepair. I felt a twinge of nostalgia for days gone by as I observed the contrasts.

Thankfully, Maureen was waiting in front of the building when I pulled up. She wore jogging tights, running shoes, and a warm-up jacket. I left my gear in the car.

"I take it we're training outdoors today?" I asked with a smile I didn't feel. We exchanged a quick embrace, and I noticed her eyes flicker toward the building's interior.

"I decided it might be best to use the weather to our advantage. I thought that a little sunshine and the spring air might do you some good, what with being cooped up at that junkyard all the time." She stepped back and examined me head to toe. "You look good, Colin. Better than I've seen you look in a while. Out of shape, maybe, but good."

I patted my gut. "Too much fast food and too little swordplay, I think. Didn't see much reason to keep my skills and conditioning up. Almost cost me my life the other night."

She pulled her long red hair back and tied it in a ponytail with a scrunchie. "No matter. We'll have you back in fighting shape in no time. You ready?"

"As I'll ever be."

She nodded and took off at a brisk pace that I struggled to match. Maureen ran us through downtown, past several old neighborhoods, and into the greenbelt and trail system that divided the town from east to west. Years ago, the city had invested in their parks system in an effort to attract Austinites to the area. It turned out to be a smart move. People in Austin loved their green spaces.

Now, the town had miles and miles of trails connecting several city parks, and it looked like Maureen intended to run them all. I followed her down a trail that took us along the river, under IH-35 and to the other side of town where the old money lived. We exited into a neighborhood of ranch-style homes and two-story mini-mansions that had just enough charm to avoid being obnoxious. We followed the broad, leaf-lined streets until we arrived at a narrow blacktop lane that trailed off into the distance. After about a mile, we finally came to a stop in a cul-de-sac below the dam.

Being part-kelpie, Maureen wasn't even breathing hard when I caught up to her. But me? I was gasping for breath. I suspected she could have run like that all day. Kelpies were shapeshifters, and preferred to spend much of their time in horse form. As with other types of shapeshifters, she retained many of the traits of her other form when in her bipedal state; in this case, great stamina and speed.

She chuckled as she scanned the area. "It was just six miles.

Time was you could have done that run in under thirty minutes."

I held up one finger. "Just a sec. Think I might puke." I took a few deep breaths and stood up. "No, it passed. You were saying?"

She walked to the edge of the road nearby, disappearing for a moment into the dense foliage beyond. She soon reappeared with two practice swords in her hands. She tossed me a waister in the shape of a longsword, which I barely managed to snag out of the air.

"I said, we have a lot of work to do." She leapt at me, swinging the wooden sword in a furious series of cuts aimed at my head, hand, knee, and stomach. I managed to parry them while backpedaling in a circle, but she kept her attacks up. Within seconds, I was breathing even harder. Maureen seemed to be barely breaking a sweat.

I was keeping her at bay with skills that I'd spent endless hours honing, but my conditioning was shit. That old military adage came to mind, that fatigue makes cowards of men. I soon became acutely aware of the fact that my arms were tiring, my lungs were burning, and my legs felt like lead. Despite the economy of my movements, it was only a matter of time before one of those cuts got through. Sure, we were practicing with wooden swords—but getting hit by a fast-moving practice sword *hurt*.

I decided to go on the offensive. I slipped outside a thrust while redirecting it to the inside. I flipped my sword around in the same motion, turning the parry into a cut at the back of her hand. She nodded and danced out of range before I could make a follow-up attack. As tired as I was, my footwork was much slower than hers—but I decided to press the offensive just the same. I stomped forward with my front foot, gliding my back leg up as smoothly as I could manage to maintain my stance and posture. With each stomp, I cut and thrust with my blade, doing my best to find an opening.

For all my efforts, it was clear that Maureen was just playing with me. I overextended myself on an ill-timed thrust, and then she was just gone. I felt a wooden blade on the side of my neck and realized she'd been moving at human speed… until now.

"A vampire won't give you time to warm-up. They'll use their superior speed in an opening attack, and if you give them the chance, you'll be the next item on the menu." She dropped the blade from my neck, and I heard her take a step back. I turned to face her and she grimaced. "Your form is rough, your conditioning has gone to hell, and your reflexes have slowed by at least half a second. Are you sure you're up to taking on this job?"

I leaned on the sword and took several ragged breaths before responding. "He killed an innocent woman—a single mom, with her kids in the next room. On my watch. I can't let it pass, Maureen."

She tilted her head and cocked an eyebrow. "Sure you can."

I wiped sweat from my brow with the back of my hand. "No, I can't. If I do, he'll kill again, and again, and again. The Circle won't stop this guy, because they either think it's one of Luther's people, or they know it isn't and they want an excuse to clear Luther's coven out. Any hunter who's worth a damn works for the Circle. And Luther says he's been trying to catch him for weeks, but this vamp has stayed two steps ahead of him. It's on me."

Maureen scowled. "I find it hard to believe that Luther can't catch a rogue vamp messing around in his territory. There's something else at work here, Colin. Something you're missing. You sure this vamp isn't fae?"

I considered the question. It was a fair one. The first vampire I'd ever killed—the first supernatural creature I'd encountered, in fact—had been fae. He'd been one of the *neamh-mairbh*, the undead, and a powerful sorcerer besides. Back then, I'd had no idea how to tell a vampire from a fae from a 'thrope. Now, it was second nature—or, at least, it should've been.

"No idea."

"You mean you didn't read him?" I shrugged. "Thought never occurred to you, did it? Sloppy. You better get your head in the game, before you face this thing. Because if you can't handle him—"

"I know, Maureen. I know what'll happen if I slip up and my Hyde-side comes out to play."

She leaned on the sword and planted a fist on her hip. "And you're sure there's no one else who might handle it?"

"None."

She hung her head slightly, then blew a stray lock of hair out of her face.

"Then I guess we'd better get back to work."

This time, I didn't manage to raise my sword quickly enough to block her attack. I received a hard rap on my elbow as punishment. I made a mental note to pick up ice and some zip-lock bags on the way home. Come tomorrow morning, I was going to need them.

6

I drove back to Austin late that night, battered and bruised. Maureen had worked me over something awful. She might have looked like your typical college co-ed, but she moved like a panther and hit like a linebacker. Still, sparring with her was just what I needed right now.

I'd stopped by my mom's place before heading home. She'd fussed over me, fed me, and mostly avoided asking about my love life. Thankfully, all my bruises were hidden—or most of them, anyway. Mom had gotten used to seeing me black and blue all the time, and rarely questioned it anymore.

When I was younger, I blamed it on roughhousing, falling out of trees, and so on. Later, my excuse was martial arts training. That one was easy, because Finnegas had required us to train in as many styles of combat as possible. It was still a ready excuse for whenever I sported a black eye or split lip.

Driving home, I considered my options for moving the case forward. I decided that I needed more info, because what I had to go on was slim. Tomorrow, I'd hit my friend Belladonna up for some intel. She worked for the Cold Iron Circle as a hunter, and had access to information I couldn't get without committing a felony or two.

Not like the Circle didn't commit any felonies to get their intel; it was just that they were so connected and well-funded, they never got caught. Where they got their money and who backed them was a mystery. All I knew was what Finnegas had told me—that their history went back centuries, all the way to medieval Europe. That, and every Circle member and recruit was human, one hundred percent. They were militantly anti-fae and anti-monster—no ifs, ands, or buts.

Their local commander hated my guts because of my curse. He thought it made me a danger to the local population. And, he was right. For that reason, I hated asking Belladonna to stick her neck out to help me.

Thankfully, it looked like I wouldn't have to ask for Belladonna's help. When I arrived back at my room, there was a manila envelope waiting for me on the other side of my door. It was sealed, had my name on the outside, and bore no other markings. I cast a cantrip to enhance my senses and scanned it for magical traps. It was free of any magical residue, but smelled like roasted coffee beans and blood. Definitely a gift from Luther.

I opened it and dumped the contents out on my makeshift desk, which was nothing more than an old wooden door that sat atop some cinder blocks. Inside sat a small stack of bills and a thumb drive. I fanned the bills with my thumb and counted fifteen hundreds.

"Shit, Luther—ever hear of small bills?" I muttered as I plugged the thumb drive into my laptop. The machine whirred to life, and I clicked to open the single folder it contained.

As I did, my phone buzzed. A text, from an unknown number.

-Luther thought you might need an advance to cover expenses. The footage is everything we could get from the night you ran into R.-

A vamp had definitely sent that text. Nobody sent texts with that kind of attention to grammar and spelling unless they were ancient. The phone buzzed again.

-If you need anything, stop by the coffee shop. Order the "special brew," and someone will contact you to provide whatever aid you require.-

Yep, gotta be a vamp. There were three files inside the folder I'd opened. I clicked the first one. It showed the camera feeds from inside the bar. I sped the video up until it showed me walking in and stacking up empty glasses. A few minutes later, Raffy and Charlene arrived. I caught a blur of movement from Raffy when they ordered their first round of drinks, which must have been when he'd drugged her. I rewound the clip and advanced it frame by frame, but the camera was too slow to catch it.

Damn it, but he's fast. I advanced to when I spilled the drink on him, and watched the footage a few times to see if it might reveal any clues. Nothing. I clicked on the next file, which was from the security cam in the alley. It showed me walking into the frame, then there was a blur and Raffy was standing behind me. I stabbed him; there was another blur, and then I shot him.

I backed the footage up. Something about the whole vignette didn't seem quite right. I enlarged the footage and played it back again, advancing it a frame at a time. *There.* The first time I stabbed at him, my elbow went through his body. At first, I thought it was a trick of the light, or that I'd missed him and stabbed through his jacket. But no, my arm passed right *through* his torso. I was sure of it.

Maybe Maureen's theory was right. Maybe this thing was fae. If so, this wouldn't be a simple stake and bake operation. Any fae vampire was double the trouble. They'd have command of all the physical attributes of a vampire, and whatever other magic they had at their disposal.

Not to mention, every fae was different. All fae had access to minor spells, such as the ability to glamour themselves to look more human. Certain kinds had innate magical talents, like the ability to shift into other forms. And higher fae often had advanced knowledge of magic. Many older fae spent centuries delving into various magical arts and practices, and they were not to be trifled with.

The Avartagh had been one such fae. He'd been a powerful sorcerer, a very old vampire—and my first kill. I'd been lucky to survive that encounter. By all rights, I should have died that day. I doubted I'd be that lucky a second time, no matter how much Irish blood ran through my veins. I'd need to come prepared this time.

My command of magic was shit compared to what most older fae could do. Hell, it was shit compared to most human magic-users who were serious about their craft. I might have been trained by a druid, but I hadn't cared much for learning magic. I'd always been more of a brawler than a magician, so my knowledge was limited to minor cantrips—spells to open locks, to help me see better in the dark, that sort of thing.

I'd always intended to go back and learn more about magic from Finnegas later, once Jesse and I had graduated from high school and were living on our own. I'd planned to do it when I had more time and all that. Only now, I couldn't stand the sight of the man. He spent all his time getting drunk or high... or both. So, the likelihood of rapidly leveling up my magical skills was about nil right now.

Thankfully, I was very good at improvising. My magical education might have been incomplete, but that didn't mean it was useless. I decided to rig a few surprises for my next meeting with Count Chocula. Hopefully, they'd be enough to even the odds and prevent a near-death experience that might bring out my Hyde-side.

But first, I needed a good night's rest. I tended to my cuts and scrapes in the warehouse bathroom, washed up, and headed back to my room. I collapsed on the bed and fell asleep immediately, but my dreams were haunted by images of Charlene—her throat savaged and torn, choking on her own blood.

7

The next day, I finished some work in the yard that Ed had left for me, then headed back to the warehouse to meet Maureen again. I was feeling pretty beat up, but I didn't feel nearly as bad as I looked. I had bruises all over my arms, legs, and torso, but they were already fading—courtesy of my genetic gifts as a born hunter. Besides a little muscle stiffness, I felt pretty good.

Maureen was already jogging away from the parking lot when I pulled up. I took the hint and locked my uncle's junker up, then headed after her. Man, that kelpie could run. She had a quarter-mile lead on me already, and that gap was increasing. I figured I knew where she was headed and decided to take it easy. No sense in wearing myself out before the sparring started.

About a mile after I hit the green belt, a pale-skinned, red-headed blur tackled me from the left side of the trail. I managed to roll with the impact, but we landed in a scramble. Somehow, she ended up on top of me, choking me with my own shirt.

Besides the lack of oxygen going to my brain, I had to admit that I didn't mind it much. Like I said, Maureen was one hot fae girl—and having her hips grinding on top of mine brought back feelings I hadn't experienced since Jesse died.

I tried to relieve the pressure from the cross-choke she had me in by squeezing her elbows together. Unfortunately, she was stronger than I was. So, I decided to just sit back and enjoy it.

That was a mistake.

Maureen leaned in close to me, chest to chest, as she sunk the choke in deeper. She dropped her head next to mine and whispered in my ear. "Keep your mind on your training, lad. I'm not here to entertain or amuse you, and I'm damn sure not going to lay your sorry ass."

I was starting to fade out, so I tapped her arm several times.

"Oh, you think that vamp is going to let you tap? Pfah." She released the choke and rolled off me before I passed out completely. I laid there for a second, letting the blood reach my brain again before I spoke.

"Sorry, Maureen. It won't happen again."

She knelt a few paces away, observing me through slitted eyes. "See that it doesn't. Not that I'm not flattered, as you've grown into a fine-looking young man. But that sort of thing will get you killed, and I don't need that on my conscience."

She stood and brushed her running tights off. "Now, get up and get your ass in gear. Every thirty seconds I have to wait at the dam'll be a set of hill sprints after we finish training."

I rolled to my knees and waited for the dizziness to subside as I watched her athletic figure race away from me. "Man, I need to get out more," I muttered, as I sprinted after her.

ROUGHLY THIRTY MINUTES LATER, I pulled to a stop at the foot of the dam, panting much like the day before—but not quite so exhausted. Maureen wasted no time at all and tossed me a practice sword before I could catch my breath. We sparred for an hour or so, and once again she had the better of me in every exchange.

Still, I could tell my reflexes were improving, and I was starting to get my rhythm and timing back as well. If I had to guess, I wouldn't be quite so bruised tonight as the night before. It was progress, and I'd take it.

After we finished, Maureen grabbed some water bottles from a cooler she'd hidden in the trees. She handed me one and regarded me with a curious look.

"So, you haven't dated at all since Jesse...?" She let her question trail off, to avoid saying what no one wanted to say.

I shook my head. "It hasn't exactly been a priority. I've been too busy with other stuff."

"Dr. Larsen told me. Trying to off yourself and failing, from what I hear. You're over that now, are you?"

I took a swig from the bottle and gave her a thumbs up. "I'm staying on my meds and doing what the doc suggested. Meditation, music, and community. Seems to be working."

"Good to know. But you need to get laid, lad—that much is obvious. Young men have needs, and you can't ignore them just because your heart is aching. Might even help with that, you know."

I wiped a drop of sweat from the tip of my nose and stared at the ground. "I know. I just..."

She squinted with one eye and gave me a frown. "You're just not ready yet?"

"Nope."

"S'all right, son. Time will heal that wounded heart. Take it from someone who has lived a sight longer than you, eh? Just hang in there and give it time."

I smiled, even though I didn't feel it. "That's the plan, right?"

Maureen returned the smile. Hers looked more heartfelt

than mine. "That's the spirit. Fake it 'til you make it, and all that."
I watched as she took the practice swords and hid them back in
the trees, along with our trash. Once she'd erased all trace of our
presence, she turned to me with an evil grin.

"You owe me three sets of hill sprints. Once you're done,
meet me back at the warehouse." She took off at a blistering
pace, her lithe legs eating up the distance with sure and steady
strides.

I cursed her silently, swearing to get even with her in a future
sparring session.

THE NEXT WEEK went much the same. I got a bit faster and less
winded, and left with fewer bruises each day. When I arrived
at the warehouse on the seventh day, the realtor's lock had
been removed and the front door was propped open. I gave
myself a minute or two to catch my breath, then nervously
marched in.

The air inside smelled musty and stale, with just the faintest
hint of old pipe smoke. The old man had loved his pipe back in
the day. The aroma brought back pleasant memories of simpler,
if not easier, times. Maureen sat just inside at the reception desk.
She finished typing something on the computer, then turned to
face me.

"Sorry—just sending a response to the city about this old
place. They're threatening to file a tax lien on it, saying it's an
eyesore and all that. Thing is, the taxes are paid up, and I've paid
every fine they've levied. I'm afraid I may have to reopen the
business, just to get them off our backs.

"Bah, but you don't want to hear about that nonsense. Probably don't even want to be here, eh?" I shrugged. "S'what I
figured. So, I'll be brief. It's been a while since you hunted

anything human or other, and I think you need a tune-up gig to get you back into the swing of things."

"What did you have in mind?"

She narrowed her eyes and crinkled her nose slightly. "Refresh my memory... did you and Jesse ever have the opportunity to hunt a fetch?"

I rubbed my neck and thought back to our hunting days. "Hmmm, can't say we did. I remember Finnegas telling us about them, but from what I remember they're rather rare—aren't they?"

She held up a finger and pointed it at me. "Indeed, they are, and for good reason. They're doppelgängers, as you'll recall—except they steal a bit of luck from the people they impersonate. It's how they power their magic, you see. And, the longer they impersonate them, the more luck they steal."

"Ah, so that explains why the people they impersonate usually die."

"Eggs-actly. Their luck goes to hell because the fetch steals it, and then one day bam! They get hit by a truck crossing the street, or a piano falls on them, or they get struck by lightning, or their pharmacist dispenses the wrong medication... well, I think you get the point."

"You want me to track a fetch down?"

She tapped the side of her nose with one finger. "A sharp one, you are. Sure enough, we seem to have recently acquired the company of one such creature in these parts. The locals aren't aware of it, mind you, but the fae 'round here talk. This fellow showed up a few weeks back, and he's been impersonating the locals to accomplish all sorts of mischief. Petty theft, running up bar tabs, dining and dashing at restaurants, and the like."

"So, you need me to catch him and run him out of town, before someone's luck runs out."

She tilted her head. "Or kill the slimy bastard—makes no difference to me. Just don't underestimate him. They're known to be sneaky little devils, and he'll stick a knife in you just as soon as he'll say hello."

"I'll keep that in mind. Any idea where he's hiding out?"

She pointed to a framed map of the town on the wall, and circled a small section with a dry-erase marker. "All the people he's impersonated so far live in this neighborhood. Chances are good he's squatting in an abandoned house or something similar. That's likely where you'll find him. And go armed, for goodness' sake."

I gave her a halfhearted salute and headed for the door. "Alright then. I guess I'm off to fetch a fetch."

8

The area Maureen had pointed out on the map was an old neighborhood. It was a mix of painstakingly restored Victorians and Craftsman-style homes, as well as shotgun houses and small cottages that were holdovers from when it had been the poorest part of town.

Home-flippers looking to make a quick buck were snatching up the older houses in the area. And because homes here were in demand, there were zero abandoned properties to search. All the unoccupied homes were either under construction or under contract, according to the signs in the yard. I found it highly unlikely that the fetch would be holed up in one of those homes —not when he could simply impersonate a local resident and live in comfort. I just hoped no one had died in the process.

Born and raised in this town, I knew most of the townies in every neighborhood. And in every small-town neighborhood, there was always one person who was a bit too nosy for their own good. On this side of town, that person would be Mrs. Schmidt, a widow whose family had lived here since the town had been founded by German settlers in the 1800s. I'd done yard work for her when I was a kid, but I hadn't spoken to her in years. As I walked the cracked paving stones to her front door, I hoped like hell that she hadn't passed on since I'd last seen her.

I pressed her doorbell button and smiled at the old-school buzzing sound it made. Several seconds later, someone cracked the door and a rheumy eye peeked out at me.

"Whatdya want? If it's work you're looking for, I already have a Mexican who does my lawn. And if you're with the Jay-Dubyas, I've been a Lutheran since the day I was birthed into this world, and I don't intend to switch religions now just to cover my bases. So, you're wasting your time."

It was definitely Mrs. Schmidt. Like many of the older townies I knew, she was ever-so-slightly racist and lacked even a hint of self-awareness regarding that fact. Institutional racism ran deep in these old towns, and while times had changed a great deal, some old folks never would. Most didn't mean any harm by it; they simply had no idea that society had changed and passed them by decades ago. Growing up in a small Texas town, I'd learned to ignore it, for the most part.

"Mrs. Schmidt? It's me, Colin. Colin McCool? I'm Leanne's son."

The eye squinted at me for a moment. "Hang on, let me get my glasses. I can't see a damned thing that's closer than five feet without them these days."

A now bespectacled eye returned to the crack, widening with recognition. The door swung open. Mrs. Schmidt stood there, leaning on a walker in a brightly-flowered muumuu dress and house shoes. Her hair was done up in curlers, and she wore a hair net over the entire affair.

I waggled my fingers at her and smiled. "Hi, Mrs. Schmidt. Long time no see."

She frowned at me, then a smile broke across her face. "Little Colin McCool, my but how you've grown. Come in, young man, come in." She turned and shuffled toward her living room, and I followed obediently, shutting the door behind us.

Mrs. Schmidt patted her hair self-consciously. "Please excuse my appearance. I have a potluck at church tonight, and there's a spry old man I've had my eye on for some time now. Planning to make my move tonight." She eased herself onto a slightly worn couch, directly in front of a TV set tuned to a game show channel. "Have a seat, child, and tell me what brings you to my door."

"Well, ma'am, I'm working for a real estate investor, helping him spot deals and opportunities in this area. He's interested in a few homes in the neighborhood, and I'm curious whether you know anyone who might consider selling. He's particularly interested in people who may have lost their jobs recently, and who might need to get out from under their mortgage."

"Sounds like a real vulture to me. Heck of a way to make a living, profiting from the misery of others. How'd you get mixed up with an outfit like that?"

"Oh, it's just something I do on the side, to save money for college. Honestly, I don't care for the people I work with—but it pays well. And occasionally, I get to help people in need."

She blew her nose into a crumpled paper towel, then stuffed it in a pocket in her muumuu. "Well, I suppose you have to do what you have to do. Times being what they are and all. Mexicans coming over the border in droves, stealing all our jobs. If they weren't so useful, I'd say throw them all in jail."

"That's a very progressive viewpoint, ma'am. Very forward-thinking of you."

"Please. It's not like I'm going to start voting Democrat. It's just that I can see the writing on the wall." She pointed to a tray full of Brach's candy on her coffee table. "Now, have some sugar while I think for a minute."

I snagged a couple of orange slices, chewing on one and pocketing two more for the road. Mrs. Schmidt scratched her leg and moved her dentures around in her mouth while she considered my question. It was rather unnerving to watch, so I kept my eyes glued to the TV set.

"Hmm... well... Sue Schulz lost her husband a while back. Tragic accident, that. The fool was driving down the highway reading a book while his electric car did the steering for him. Ran right into a semi—flattened him and that fancy car like a pancake. No, but she doesn't need the money. Settlement should keep her in yoga pants and lattes for life, the little hussy.

"Then there's Pete Thompson across the street. Used to work on cars, but he lost all his fingers in a tragic bull-riding accident. The idiot got drunk and thought he could last eight seconds. He got tossed, but his hand got stuck in the rope. Popped all four fingers clean off. I figure his insurance checks should be running out soon, so you might approach him.

"Then there's that Middle-Eastern fellow down the way. Sanjay, Sanjah, Sanjan—something to that effect. I can't ever get those people's names right. Not like any one of them can speak proper English, so I don't feel bad about mangling their names a smidgen. He's been acting funny lately, hanging around his house all day and not going into work, avoiding his neighbors, that sort of thing. I called the sheriff and told them to investigate him for terrorism. Anybody who gets shifty like that overnight must be planning something terrible.

"Anyway, he must be hard up for cash about now, because I'm sure he's lost his job already. And if he does try to blow something up, well... your boss ought to be able to get his house dirt cheap on auction. After he goes to jail, that is. Unless he's one of those suicide bombers—but either way, it ought to sell cheap. Kind of like those meth lab houses. Bound to be full of chemicals and whatnot, besides stinking of all those exotic spices he cooks with. Every time he makes dinner I can smell it all the way down the street. Damned nuisance, if you ask me."

And this is why I moved to Austin, I thought. "That's great, Mrs. Schmidt. You wouldn't happen to have an address for Mr. Sanjay?"

"Don't need one. His is the red brick house down on the corner, the one with the pagan statues in the flower bed. Can't miss it. And when you go down there, tell him to quit stinking up the neighborhood."

Mrs. Schmidt's house smelled like cabbage and mothballs. I figured a little curry would be an improvement, but I kept my mouth shut as I stood and looked at my phone. "Oh, look at the time. I'd best be going, but I want to thank you, ma'am. You've been a tremendous help."

She waved a hand at me and dropped it back on the couch's armrest. "Bah, it's nothing. Besides, after that horrible accident your girlfriend was in, well... I'm just glad to know you're doing alright."

I forced a smile. "I'm getting there, Mrs. Schmidt. I'm getting there."

Her expression was one hundred percent false sympathy, and I knew she'd be gossiping about me later. "Excuse me for not getting up, young man, but my show is coming on. Don't forget to tell San-jiminy to close his windows when he cooks."

She turned her eyes to the TV set, and I locked the door for her as I exited the house. Mrs. Schmidt might have been a bigoted old busybody, but she'd been good to my mom after my dad had died. That was the thing with people. Morally speaking, most weren't all good or all bad, but instead occupied the spaces between.

But when it came to the fae, they were all bad in my opinion. As far as I was concerned, killing an unseelie fae was just like squashing a black widow, or cutting the head off a poisonous snake. Even if the thing had no intention of harming you, it might down the road—so it was best to end it before it ended you.

Not like I had any room to talk. I'd killed my own girlfriend. Or rather, the curse had. I could blame the fae for it, and I did. But ultimately, I was the one that did the killing. And now I had to live with it.

After I left Mrs. Schmidt's house, I walked back to the car and dug around for a few items inside my Craneskin Bag. Then I took a quick detour across the street, leaving an envelope with most of the cash Luther had advanced me in Mr. Thompson's mail slot. I had been classmates with his daughter, and I knew her dad was helping to pay her way through school. I figured they needed the money more than I did—and besides, I had more coming.

Once that was done, I cut through Mr. Thompson's yard on my way to the alley and headed for Mr. Sanjay's house.

9

I didn't know Mr. Sanjay, but a quick look on social media told me he was single with no kids. He was also employed as an engineer at one of the larger tech companies in town. He was the perfect target for a doppelgänger. I was certain I'd found my fetch, and seeing Mr. Sanjay's yard confirmed my suspicion. The grass hadn't been mown in weeks, and there were bags of trash piled up outside the back door.

Thus far, I hadn't a clue why this fetch had decided to take up residence in such a small town, where the likelihood of being caught was much higher than in a large metropolis like Austin. And I could only speculate as to what his game was in impersonating Mr. Sanjay and taking over his life. Was he hiding out from someone or something? Did this fetch travel from town to town, stealing the lives of humans and moving on before he got caught?

Or was he just really, really bad at being a doppelgänger? Just as humans had dumb criminals, the supernatural world had dumb monsters. In fact, dumb monsters were sort of the bread and butter of hunter work. While people who were clued into the world beneath were rare, there was always someone who needed a nasty fae or other supernatural creature dealt with. And, as it so happened, monsters who revealed their presence to humans tended to be the dumbest of the dumb. Or the most vicious. Or both.

Any way you sliced it, stupid creatures paid the bills. As for how we got these jobs, word tended to get around. People would start asking questions in online forums and social media groups that focused on the weird and unexplained. "Say, does anyone know how to get rid of a herd of three-foot humanoid lizards?" That sort of thing. Freelance hunters tended to monitor that sort of chatter online. We'd reach out to whoever had made the post, find out if it was legit, and then offer our services.

The Circle was too busy guarding humanity against whatever major threats they deemed worthy of their time to handle most of these cases. Hauntings, infestations, poltergeists, supernatural abductions, and the like were beneath them, and hardly even worth their attention. So, hunters like me took those jobs. The pay wasn't always good, but lots of monsters hoarded money and valuables, so that tended to make up for it. The life of a hunter could be very, very rewarding.

If you didn't get killed or maimed so badly that it ended your career.

Of course, I wasn't getting paid for this job. This one was a freebie, and that was okay. I hated the fae—hated them for what they did to humans and what they'd done to me. I'd been cursed by a fae sorceress, and that curse had caused Jesse's death. So, I had no problem taking out any rogue fae who didn't know how to stay in their lane.

None whatsoever.

I snuck up to the back door through knee-high grass, mindful that I didn't accidentally step on a rattlesnake or coral snake along the way. Snakes loved neighborhoods, because they always had plenty of small prey to feed on like rats, mice, baby rabbits, and squirrels. Also, some supernatural creatures attracted animals like spiders, snakes, and bats, so you had to be mindful of that when hunting certain creatures. If people knew what sort of vermin were living right under their noses— including the supernatural kind—well, let's just say there'd be a lot more Xanax prescriptions being written.

Once I got to the back door I listened for a few minutes, then checked to see if it was unlocked. No sense in using magic if it wasn't warranted. Unfortunately, this fetch liked his privacy, so the place was buttoned up tight. I checked the entrance for magical wards—nada. I cast a cantrip on the door to unlock it, then waited to see if the spell had alerted the fetch.

After a few more minutes of silence, I slowly turned the knob and cracked the door. The odor of rotten food, curry, and unwashed human hit me, and I heard a radio or TV set playing somewhere toward the front of the house. *Good.* The noise would cover the sound of my movements.

I duck-walked inside and closed the door as quietly as possible. I was now in the kitchen. *Great, the second busiest room in the house.* I needed to move before I got spotted. I drew my pistol and screwed a noise suppressor on the barrel. No sense in freaking the neighbors out if this job got nasty. Since I was dealing with a fae creature, I had the gun loaded with hollow point rounds tipped with iron pellets. They wouldn't kill most fae—not unless I got a good head shot—but they'd damned sure slow them down.

I heard someone stir on the other side of the wall. It was either my target or his victim. I decided to investigate and crept out of the kitchen, into a short corridor that led to a doorway. Probably the master bedroom. I snuck around the corner and slowly opened the door.

The room smelled of urine and human excrement. Inside, Mr. Sanjay was lying on the floor in a puddle of his own filth.

He'd been restrained and gagged with a shit-ton of duct tape and telephone line, and he looked like he'd been beaten. As I entered the room, his eyes snapped open and zeroed in on me.

I held a finger to my lips. "It's alright, Mr. Sanjay. I'm here to help." He immediately began squirming and grunting wildly. I crept forward to calm him down. "Mr. Sanjay, I need you to be quiet. I fully intend to release you, but first I need to neutralize your captor. Is he in the house?"

Mr. Sanjay's head bobbed up and down. His eyes got wide as saucers as they darted back and forth, from me to over my shoulder and back again.

I rolled out of the way, just as a meat cleaver split the air horizontally where my head had just been. I spun as I rolled, and came up firing at Mr. Sanjay's double. The resemblance wasn't just uncanny; it was perfect. Well, except for the pitch-black eyes that regarded me with the deepest hatred imaginable.

I shot the thing in the shoulder and leg. It dropped the cleaver and fell to one knee, clutching its shoulder with its uninjured hand, and using its wounded arm to staunch the blood flow from the bullet hole in its thigh.

"Ah, fecking hell! Why can't you hunters use swords and spears anymore like proper warriors? Gah, and bullets laced with cold iron as well. It'll take me forever to heal up from this."

The fetch's Irish brogue was shockingly incongruent, coming from Mr. Sanjay's mouth. I wisely kept my pistol trained on him as I stood.

"Who says you're going to have the opportunity to heal from this?" I asked as I stared the fetch down.

He chuckled. "You'll let me live if you want to keep this idjit from babbling about rakshashas and davanas all over the place. Been trying to tell him for weeks now that I'm Irish, but the chap won't listen. Had to tie him up because he kept trying to escape.

Nearly had to bust his damned head open just to keep him quiet."

"I suppose this is where you try to convince me that you're just another harmless fae, a victim of the spread of modern human society and the advance of technology."

He rolled his eyes. "Far from it. This human's life is as meaningless to me as a bug I might squish underfoot. No, I'm no innocent—at least, not by your measure."

I began to increase pressure on the pistol's trigger. The fetch raised his hands up defensively.

"Now, now—before you go and do something rash, at least allow me to parley for me life. I can help you, hunter. Honest."

I knew he wasn't lying. How? Fae couldn't lie, but they could dissemble. It was mind-blowing, how easily they could trick a human without ever speaking an untrue word. Still, you never knew what sort of info you might get out of a fae creature, so I decided to play along.

"Go on. Tell me *exactly* how you can help me."

"Well, for starters, I can cast a spell on Mr. Sanjay over there, and make him forget this all ever happened."

I looked back at Sanjay, who was sweating bullets. "We'll see. What else?"

"I have information! I mean, did you stop to wonder what the hell I'm doing out here in Bumfucked, Texas?"

I cleared my throat. "The thought did cross my mind. Enlighten me. Why are you working a mark out here in the sticks, when the city is just a short drive down the road?"

"Ah-ha! Now you're asking the right questions. I'll tell you why," he said as he straightened against the wall. "Because I got forced out."

"Forced out of Austin? What, did you piss Maeve off?"

He frowned. "I daresay not. I'm as loyal to the queen as ever. No, I was forced out of business."

I sat down on Mr. Sanjay's bed and reached over to pull the tape off his mouth, keeping an eye on the fetch. "I'm sorry, Mr. Sanjay, but this is a story I have to hear. Can I trust you to keep quiet while I converse with your evil double over here?"

Poor Mr. Sanjay immediately began babbling in broken English and Hindi. Apparently, his experiences over the previous few weeks had been too much for him. I replaced the tape, muffling his ramblings for the time being.

"Alright, fetch. You have two minutes to convince me that I shouldn't put a bullet in your head."

10

Over the next fifteen minutes or so, the fetch told me an interesting tale. He'd had a thriving "business" in Austin, working as an inside man for various criminal crews on cons and heists. Apparently, his skills had been in high demand among non-fae supernatural criminals—at least until recently. Supposedly, a charm-worker by the name of Cécile had moved into town and ruined his business. She sold glamours to anyone with the cash—or favors in trade—to pay for them.

Where this Cécile chick had come from, he didn't know. But, apparently, she was bad business—in more ways than one.

"So, I go to the bitch to appeal to her better nature. You know, to tell her she's ruining my business and putting me in the poor house. And you know what she does? She says, 'Tough shite, ya dope.' And laughs at me."

"And then what happened?"

He wiped something from his eye with a knuckle and scowled. "She put a hex on me, is what she did. On me! Cursed me luck to turn sour, and now I gotta stay in character all the time, siphoning luck off geebags like this one. The nerve! Had my old crew chase me outta town too. Told them if they didn't, they'd never get another of her spells again."

"Uh-huh. And where can I find this Cécile?"

"She operates out of the back room at a joint called The Hammer and Anvil."

"Strange name for a fae bar."

He shrugged. "The place is run by a werebear—some big Nordic guy who thinks he's the second coming of Thor. He's a right prick, but he tolerates fae if they watch their manners. I think he might be getting the ride from the witch, so watch yerself if you pay her a visit."

I nodded. "Anything else I should know?"

"No, nothing that comes to mind."

"Give me a second—what was your name again?"

"Manny."

"Alright, Manny. I have to check in with my handler, then we'll figure out how to handle this."

I called Maureen. "Yeah, I found him. Uh-huh. Yeah, just the one witness. Gotcha, see you in a few."

I ended the call and shot the fetch in the head. Mr. Sanjay started going nuts. I turned to him and sighed.

"Relax! I'm not going to hurt you, but I can't have you screaming and yelling and getting your neighbors over here. So, we're just going to sit tight until my friend shows up, and she's going to take care of everything. Alright?"

He nodded, his eyes plastered to the pistol in my hand. I realized I'd been gesturing with it as I'd talked. I sighed again and tucked it in my Craneskin Bag, just in case someone had happened to hear gunfire and came to investigate. Suppressors muffled the sound of a gunshot, but they didn't completely silence it. All that crap you see in movies and on TV, where someone fires a silenced pistol and it sounds like a Nerf gun? Yeah, bullshit.

Mr. Sanjay calmed down, and I sat on the bed next to him in awkward silence while Manny bled all over the carpet. Then he began to shift back into his natural state, which was kind of reminiscent of Odo from *DS9*. It made me wonder if one of the special effects artists on the show had been clued in to the world beneath.

A few minutes later, I heard a knock at the front door. I pulled my pistol and crept to the entryway, peeking out the blinds to make sure it was Maureen. I opened the door for her, careful not to let anyone spot me as she walked inside.

"Oh, man, am I glad to see you. That guy is totally freaked out. I'm thinking that maybe I shouldn't have shot his double in front of him. He was pretty traumatized already."

Maureen cocked an eyebrow. "Ya think? Show me where the body is so we can get this over with. I have an appointment for a hot stone massage and a facial that I don't want to miss."

I headed to the master bedroom with Maureen in tow. "I didn't think you fae had to worry about that stuff."

"You forget, I'm only half-fae. So, I age. Just not as quickly as a human, or as slowly as a full-blood fae. Besides that, there's nothing wrong with a girl pampering herself every now and again."

"Hey, I'm not judging." I entered the bedroom and almost slipped in a large puddle of pinkish goo, which I assumed had once been Manny. "Oh, that's so gross. Gah, and it stinks too!"

Maureen snickered. "Try not to track it all over the place, because I'm the one that's going to have to spell this place clean." She pointed at poor Mr. Sanjay in the corner. "I take it that's our victim?"

"Yeah, that's him."

She muttered an incantation and wiggled her fingers in intricate patterns. Mr. Sanjay immediately fell into a deep sleep.

"Huh. You're going to have to show me how you do that," I quipped as I wiped my shoes off on Mr. Sanjay's carpet.

"You might've already learned if you'd paid more attention to your magical studies."

"Meh, I'm more of the physical type."

She tsked. "You won't always have someone around to clean up your messes. You'll need to finish your training at some point... that is, if you intend to keep taking jobs like this."

"Naw. This is a one-time deal. After this, I'm through."

"If you say so. Help me get this tape off him, and let's get him undressed. He's going to need a bath and a shave before I bring him back around."

"For real?"

She frowned. "If you want to do this right, it has to look good."

I sighed and got to work. We spent the better part of an hour cleaning Mr. Sanjay up and getting him dressed, during which time we discussed what I'd learned from Manny. After we were done we left Mr. Sanjay on his couch with the TV on.

"You sure he won't remember anything?" I asked.

"Not a thing. I learned from the best. He'll wake up thinking he's been sick for the past several weeks. I already hacked the human resources department at his employer's and put him on convalescent leave, retroactive to the first day he missed work."

"Think it'll hold water?"

She stretched and yawned. "You'd be surprised what people will overlook to dismiss the inexplicable. Now, don't you have a witch to visit?"

"You think she might have something to do with this vamp I'm hunting down?"

Maureen looked at Mr. Sanjay for a moment, tapping a finger on her chin. In a flurry of motion, she rearranged his arms and propped his head up with a pillow.

"That's better." She stood straight again and noticed the baffled look on my face. "I didn't want him to wake up with a crick in his neck. Oh, don't tell me you've never had one. Absolutely horrendous. And in answer to your question—yes, I do. Call it a hunch. Trust me, it's worth checking out."

"Alright, noted. I'll stop by there tonight after I go home and clean up."

"Good man. Just be careful and mind your manners. The werebear will be the least dangerous of the two."

"Roger that. Anything else I should know?"

"Shore up your wards before you head over there. And call me to let me know what happens."

"Yes, Mom."

"Call me that again and I'll be the one hexing you," she hissed.

I waved my hands in the air. "Whoa, alright, alright! Geez. I meant it as a compliment."

She squeezed the bridge of her nose and sighed. "Dear boy, you do have so much to learn about women."

11

After a quick shower and a change of clothes, I hopped on my scooter and headed to The Hammer and Anvil. It turned out to be one of those new hipster bars on the east side, located in an area that was quickly becoming a concrete jungle of lofts and condominiums.

Neighborhood joints like this one provided their customers with the illusion they were slumming when they really weren't. While the place had a sort of kitschy-grunge vibe, it was really just another yuppie bar for millennials who worked for the man but wanted to pretend like they still fought the power. Whenever I heard native Austinites talk about the "old" Austin, I couldn't help but think that it was places like this that were ruining the city.

The bar was located in an old cinder block gas station with a couple additions off its side and back. The faux-rusted tin roof gave it an almost authentic roadhouse vibe, and the blues tracks blasting from the outdoor speakers in the beer garden weren't half-bad. While I sat on my scooter scoping the place out, they played a little B.B. King, a few SRV tunes, and even some John Lee Hooker.

Then they fucked it up by mixing in some White Stripes—the blues equivalent of pop punk. What a dick move. I hated the owner already.

But I wasn't out there to write a review of the place. I scoped it out in the magical spectrum, and yeah, there was some hinky shit going on in there. For one, a lot of the patrons going in and out of the place were definitely not human. I saw some fae, a few 'thropes, and at least one vamp mixed in with the crowd.

That in itself wasn't weird, since supernatural humanoids had to mingle with humans if they wanted to enjoy the benefits of human society. What was weird was how fast they were coming and going. While the human patrons tended to show up and stick around, the supernatural types didn't delay. They'd enter and leave within the span of a few minutes.

Also, there was a magical blank spot in the back addition. Everywhere else, I read the usual signs and signals you got with a monster or fae-owned business. There were wards and spells to protect against the usual crap—hexes, hauntings, and the like —but that area of the bar was *dead*. Not only was there no magic emanating from it; there was nothing coming out of there.

So, that room was either dimensionally displaced, or someone was shielding it with some serious juice.

"Shit," I said as I stomped out the cigarette I hadn't been smoking. I didn't actually care for the habit at all, but it made for a good excuse to loiter outside places while you were scoping them out. Stand around doing nothing and you looked creepy and suspicious; stand around puffing on a cigarette, and you just looked like another nicotine addict.

I dug around inside my Craneskin Bag to make sure I had my silver-etched sword, a gun loaded with silver bullets, and my war club close at hand. The sword and pistol were for the were-bear, and the club was for the charm-worker. It was fae-made and packed a hell of a punch. If she got cheeky, it'd do.

I pulled off my jacket and slung the Bag over my shoulder, then put the jacket back on and walked into the bar. Inside, it looked like an episode of *Vikings* had mated with a Chili's and exploded all over the walls. There were old street signs and other carefully-curated pieces of junk and antiques on the walls, along with several medieval weapons that looked to be the real deal. If a bar fight ever broke out in here, it was going to get nasty, fast.

But the place was clean, and it didn't smell like stale beer and piss. According to the neon dry erase board behind the bar, they were having a one-dollar pint special on a local amber ale. Figuring there was no reason to avoid mixing work and pleasure, I sidled up to the bar and took a seat.

A minute later, a huge muscular dude with long, surfer-blonde hair pulled back in a ponytail came walking out from the kitchen. He carried cases of longnecks, probably flexing a lot more than was necessary for the task. I could practically hear the group of co-eds down the bar from me swoon as he set the beers down. Manny hadn't been kidding. This guy looked exactly like Chris Hemsworth.

I hated him even more.

The guy flirted with the co-eds for a minute, while I sat there with a twenty between my fingers. He glanced down the bar at me and kept on flirting.

Fuck it. I don't need a beer that badly, anyway. I stood up and walked into his line of sight behind the girls.

"Say, do you have a restroom around here?" Chris Hemsworth ignored me and kept chatting with the co-eds. "Around back, then? Super."

I left him to his groupies and hooked a left around the corner, passing the bathrooms and heading for an unmarked door with a deadbolt. I checked it out for spells, and sure enough, it was warded. A little magical fiddling took care of that, and I cast another cantrip to unlock it.

Nothing happened.

I tried it again. Still nothing. I wondered if I'd missed a protective spell in my rush to nullify the first one I'd spotted, then it hit me. I looked around to be sure no one was watching me and tried the door.

Unlocked, of course.

I sighed and cracked it open, checking to make sure the space beyond was empty. I ducked inside and locked the door behind me. I was in a short hallway that ended in a curtained doorway roughly ten feet away. Based on my earlier scan of the premises, that was where the dead spot was.

"The spell on the door is just to let me know someone is here to see me," a dusky voice said from behind the curtain. "You're obviously not a customer, but you may as well come in just the same."

I walked ahead, cautiously parting the curtains. The room beyond was dark, with only a few candles to light the space. An attractive, light-skinned black woman sat with her legs crossed on a dark leather and chrome office couch. A low glass coffee table sat in front of her, along with two matching leather chairs to either side. The room looked as though it had been set up to receive guests, much like any formal sitting area you might have found in a modern home.

The woman wore a black silk cheongsam with a gold flower pattern. Her dress showed off sculpted arms and shoulders, as well as toned calves that ended in black high-heeled pumps. Her hair fell in wavy curls, flapper-style, to just above shoulder-length. It framed her delicate features in the most flattering manner possible. She looked just like any beautiful, well-heeled professional out for a night on the town.

And, it was all an illusion. I had to strain to see through the glamour, and nearly gasped when I saw the real woman behind it. Her skin was weathered and wrinkled, her limbs were gnarled and twisted, and her cat-like eyes glowed red in the darkness. She was nearly bald, except for a few stray wisps of hair on her liver-spotted head. Most disturbing of all, though, were her teeth. Each one had been filed to a needle-sharp point. When she smiled and ran her tongue over those chompers, I got a chill down my spine.

A soucouyant, or one of the variants, more than likely. A literal bloodsucking witch. *Interesting.*

"You must be Cécile."

She set her drink down on the table and extended her arms out to rest on the couch back, giving me a visual appraisal. I didn't know if she was sizing me up as an interloper, a potential bedmate, or a meal. Finally, after several long uncomfortable seconds of silence, she spoke.

"Well, you're not with the Circle. And I can see you aren't fooled by my disguise, so that means you're either a rival magic-user whose toes I've stepped on, or a hunter. Which is it?"

I crossed my arms, using the motion to slip my hand inside the Bag beneath my jacket. This could get ugly, fast—and I didn't want to be caught off guard by someone who probably worked magic like I worked a blade.

"A little of both, actually, although I don't have a beef with you." *Not yet, anyway.* "I'm just here for some information."

"About?"

"A rogue vampire who's been hunting around town. One who may not be everything he appears, either."

She picked up her glass and swirled its contents. "I see. Well, I have many clients, so you'll have to be more descriptive if you want a useful answer."

I almost didn't catch her casting the spell, as she did it so artfully. But as she swirled her drink, her fingers made minute gestures against the glass—so subtle they were almost imperceptible. I switched my vision into the magical spectrum and immediately saw that the contents of the glass were glowing with energy.

I began to pull my war club from the Bag, just as the witch took a swig of the drink and spat it at me like a circus fire breather. The atomized liquid transformed into a fireball in midair, then it hurtled straight at my head.

"Aw, shit," I hissed as I ducked and rolled out of the way. I tracked the fireball as it hit the wall, and watched it dissipate into sparks and mist. *An illusion.*

I came up to my feet, but she was gone. I quickly searched the room, looking behind the couch and chairs, and in every corner and cranny. The only exit was the one I'd entered through, and as far as I could tell she hadn't gone past me.

"Oh, you're good," I said to the empty room.

"You have no idea," a manly voice boomed from behind me. I turned around in time to see Chris Hemsworth barrel through the curtains. He looked pissed—and considering the short war hammer he was smacking into his palm, I could tell he wasn't here to get me that beer.

12

B ecause he was blocking the only exit, I circled around the room to place the couch and table between us. I inclined my head toward him. "Since it looks like we're about to butt heads, how about some introductions all around?"

He pointed a thumb at his chest. "Cade Valison. I own this place."

"Váli's-son? Are you shitting me?" He smirked as if to say, *what of it?* "Alrighty then. Colin McCool, freelance hunter."

"Ah, the druid-trained hunter. I've heard of you. I'm not impressed."

"Well, I only heard about you a few hours ago, so ditto. You want to tell me where the witch went?"

"Not in the slightest. And I think it's time you left my bar, cretin."

I tongued my cheek as I considered my next move. He was big, probably a hell of a lot stronger than me, and that hammer he wielded had "magic weapon" written all over it. I decided to see what he was about. It never hurt to try to talk your way out of a situation, although he did deserve a beating for his taste in music.

"Cretin? Are you for real?" I shook my head. "Never mind. Answer me one question and I'll leave peacefully."

"You'll leave whenever I throw you out," he replied. "But I can't see the harm in conversing a bit before I knock you senseless."

"Hospitality before an ass-beating. Must be a Viking thing. Here in Texas, we just skip the talk and go right to the ass-kicking."

He tilted his head and hitched his shoulders. "I enjoy a good brawl just as much as the next marauder, but I'm not completely without manners."

"Not much opportunity for that these days. Marauding, I mean."

He sighed. "Thus, the bar. The markup on liquor is the closest I can get to the spoils of war in this day and age. That and the occasional bar fight almost make it worth it."

"A bar fight among these bearded yuppies? Seriously?"

He shrugged slightly. "It's rare, but it happens."

Valison flipped his hammer in the air, catching it after it made several revolutions. He did it twice, effortlessly. He knew what he was doing with that thing, that was for sure. "Now that the small talk is out of the way, can we speed this up? I'm growing bored with you, and my fingers itch for violence."

I spun my war club between my fingers as I replied, just to get his goat. He wasn't the only one who could show off. "Fine. Tell me, what's a werebear doing hanging out with a witch? And why are you letting her operate out of your club?"

He leaned against the wall, kicking a foot up to rest behind him as he laid the war hammer on his shoulder. "I'm not a werebear, I'm a berserker. Austin being a rather peaceful city, I rarely get to let that side run wild. And without an outlet for my more violent tendencies, I get a little..."

"Edgy? Peckish? Bloated and crampy?"

He barely reacted to my wisecrack. This guy had no sense of humor at all. "I was going to say *murderous*. It takes time to set up a new identity, a new life. I've grown tired of having to start over again, every time I kill someone. She is my solution. The witch provides me with potions and charms that calm me down, and I let her use this room to conduct her business. So long as she leaves my regular customers alone, I'm happy."

"Why not move somewhere... I dunno... rougher and more violent?"

"Have you not seen the women in this town? This bar is a magnet for nubile young co-eds. And the sexual mores today! Why, in my day..."

I waved my hands in front of me. "Whoa, hold on there, R. Kelly. I get it—you're a skirt-chaser. Point taken." I leaned on the club like a cane as I continued. "And I get that whole 'wanting to avoid losing control and killing random people thing'—believe me, I do. But c'mon, you have to know that she's working with some pretty shady characters."

"That's none of my business. And none of yours, either."

"I think she's working with a vampire. One that's been killing humans left and right."

He kicked off the wall and stood with his knees slightly bent, in a sort of loose fighting stance that told me this wasn't his first rodeo—not by a long shot. "I've lived for hundreds of years. What are a few human lives to me? Humans breed like rabbits and they're fragile as glass. If a creature that's higher on the food chain decides to kill a few to survive, that is merely the natural order at work. It is no concern of mine."

Yeah, I'm going to enjoy kicking this guy's ass. I stopped twirling the club and hefted it in my right hand, pointing it at him for emphasis. "You know, I was willing to let the White Stripes thing go. Anyone can be forgiven for ruining a perfectly good blues playlist with a clunker or two. I mean, you gotta throw that stuff in to please your patrons, right?"

The berserker shrugged. "I happen to like The White Stripes."

"Seriously? As in 'like-like,' or you won't turn the dial if one of their songs comes on the radio?" He gave me a confused look, so I waved the question away. "Never mind. I can even forgive blowing me off at the bar to get a phone number—really, that one can be chalked up to observing the dude code.

"But you used to be human, once. And the fact that you see all those people who pay your bills and keep you in ponytail thongs and chest waxing sessions as expendable, well... that I just can't forgive."

"I am only half-human and a demi-god. Your threats and the people you protect mean nothing to me."

I rolled my eyes. "Whatever. Doesn't mean you can't get your ass kicked."

"You talk too much, druid, and think too highly of yourself. I believe I'll teach you some humility, along with some manners." He slapped his hammer against his palm.

"I'm no druid. Now, are we going to dance, or just hurl idle threats?"

He lunged and leapt over the coffee table as he swung that hammer like Thor himself. I sidestepped and struck him across the ribs, then followed through with a backhanded blow that he almost casually blocked with his hammer.

As the two weapons collided, a thunderclap and subsequent shockwave threw me across the room. I bounced off the wall and landed on one knee. By the time I'd collected myself, Valison was walking around the couch, taking his sweet time about it. It didn't even look like the shot I'd landed on his ribs had fazed him.

He has to be wearing armor. I exerted my will to see through any illusion or magic on him. Sure enough, he wore a set of lamellar armor, not plainclothes. A chest piece covered his entire torso and shoulders, and he wore sturdy metal bracers over his forearms and wrists. The whole getup was hidden by a glamour, one I assumed the witch had cast.

"Sweet hammer," I commented.

"Thanks," he replied. "It was a gift from my father. Not as good as my uncle's, but better than that stick you carry."

"Meh, it was designed to kill fae, not demi-gods. Still, it'll do the trick," I said as I rose to my feet. "That armor you're wearing isn't half-bad, either. But you know the problem with wearing armor?"

"I'm sure you're about to enlighten me, mortal."

I smiled. "It only protects what it covers," I said as I ducked under a vicious hammer blow meant to crush my skull.

I countered his attack with a quick *witik* to his kneecap, a whipping strike I'd learned in the martial art of kali. When done properly, it was too fast to block. It connected. On impact, the bone and cartilage in his knee shattered with a satisfying crunch. As the leg collapsed and his weight shifted, I used the rebound motion to turn the strike into an *abaniko*, or fan strike. I aimed the blow at his temple, knowing he'd raise his hammer to block it.

Nope, not falling for that again. At the last moment, I changed the trajectory of the attack and struck his elbow, which was unprotected by his bracers. It shattered just as his knee had, and the berserker dropped his hammer to the floor, clutching his elbow with his free hand.

Rather than finishing him off, I stood back and watched as he slid down to the floor in agony.

"Huh. Seems to me like the whole demi-god thing is overrated."

He gritted his teeth as he hissed a reply. "Fortunate for you that I'm currently under the witch's spell, and my berserk nature is suppressed. Things would not have gone in your favor, were I in full possession of my powers."

"Sucks for you." I slapped the club in my hand and regarded it with appreciation. "Not too bad for a stick, eh? Now, I think it's time we had us a serious chat about this witch, and where I might find her."

13

Mr. "I Am A Demi-God With Great Hair" refused to give me any information—at least until I offered to smash his other kneecap... and then did exactly that.

Of course, he threatened me with eternal enmity, blah, blah, blah. Whatever. I'd killed a "god" before—or, at least, my Hyde-side had—so I knew what real power was like. Cade Valison was tough, and hell if I wanted to face him when he went berserk. But he was nothing compared to the Caoránach.

I did consider taking him out instead of leaving him to seek revenge later. Technically, he was a monster and not human. From what Finnegas had told me, all the deities from folklore and legend were cut from the same cloth. The Tuatha, the Norse pantheon, Greek and Roman deities—they all had similar powers and similar flaws. And they all loved fucking with humans.

That made them fair game in my book.

But I didn't want some Norse deity tracking me down for killing his kid. Which was why I left him there to moan and heal after I was done with him. Was it a tactical error? Maybe. But I had whipped his ass fair and square, so there was always the possibility he'd leave it alone.

Fat chance, but still.

After I finished interrogating Cade, I tied him up with a mess of parachute cord and duct tape. I hid him behind the couch and locked and warded the door on my way out. Eventually someone would find him—hopefully just not before I hit the witch's hideout.

Once that was done, I headed over to the coffee shop for some caffeine and to let Luther's crew know I needed help. I figured I was close to finding the vamp, and if so, I wanted some backup. Plus, it wouldn't hurt to update my client on how things were going with the case.

Luther wasn't around, so after ordering the "special brew"—man, that vampire knew how to roast coffee beans—I waited to see if any of his employees would speak to me. After a few minutes of being pointedly ignored, I decided I'd better act on the intel Cade had given me.

Just as I was heading out of the cafe, two hunters from the Cold Iron Circle blocked my path.

The Circle had its headquarters right down the street—in a glitzy, upscale glass high-rise that looked like just another downtown Austin office building. Unbeknownst to the typical Austin resident, the office workers bustling in and out the front doors of that high-rise were actually support staff for the most well-funded and dangerous paramilitary organization in the supernatural world.

The Circle had been a major pain in my side for months now. They'd been harassing me ever since I'd moved to Austin. From what I gathered, they considered me public enemy number one—since I carried a fae curse that made me a walking, talking weapon of mass destruction.

What these dickheads didn't know, and what I couldn't seem to get them to understand, was that their constant harassment was only increasing the chances of my curse triggering. And if one of them tried to take me out? Then that other side of me would come out to play.

I held my hands up as I exited the café, smiling as I made eye contact with each of the thugs in turn. They were dressed like a couple of clichés, wearing tactical cargo pants, compression shirts, desert combat boots, and photographer's vests—which were intended to conceal the various firearms and bladed weapons that each Circle member carried. One was shorter, slimmer, and blonde, while the other was taller, more muscular, and bald. They also wore mirrored aviator sunglasses and looked like a couple of private military contractors pulling security duty in Mosul.

"Hey, fellas, how's it hanging? Burn down any magic forests lately? Such a shame that we're not still living in the Dark Ages —must be hard to get all your raping and pillaging in, what with mundane law enforcement looking down on that sort of thing."

Skinny spoke first. "So, druid, we hear you're in cahoots with the vamps now. You turn Renfield, or what?"

I ignored the comment and attempted to walk past them, but they closed ranks and blocked my way. I dropped my chin to my chest and sighed. "Fellas... come on now. You remember what happened to the last hunter-mage team that tried to shake me down. Let's not make a scene, shall we?"

Baldy chimed in. "Yeah, we remember. Those guys are our squad mates, and you made them the laughing stock around the locker room." He stabbed me in the chest with a thick meaty finger. "And we don't appreciate it when shitheads like you make us look bad."

I backed up a half-step and angled myself so I could vault the rail and have space to move if things got ugly. I didn't like the fact that they had me boxed-in, and berated myself for not paying better attention to my surroundings.

"Tell you what. Luther makes a mean frozen mochaccino"—I held up my drink to prove it—"so what do you say I treat you boys to a round, on me?"

The smaller one sniffed and twitched his nose. I figured he was the mage, since baldy had to be the muscle. If they moved on me, I'd have to take him out first. "Shut your trap, druid. You're not going to talk yourself out of this one. We're going to make you pay for what you did to Davis and Simpson, and there's not a damned thing you can do about it."

I raised my hands in the air and shrugged. "Hey, what's a little bladder incontinence between friends? How was I to know that your commander would show up right when my spell made your buddies piss their pants? And besides, it's not like I blasted them with a lightning bolt or something. It was just a little harmless cantrip to get them to back off."

Baldy clenched his fists. "Because of that little stunt, our squad got shit duty for a week. I had to miss going to Vegas for SHOT Show because of you. And now, it's time for payback."

I took a sip of my drink before responding. "You sure we can't talk this out?"

Blondie shook his head. "Uh-uh, not a chance. Any last words?"

"Eeny, meeny..." I said in a high-pitched voice.

The two morons looked at each other. "What the fuck is wrong with this guy?"

I made my voice go even higher. "Miny... hey, Moe!" I shouted as I kicked Blondie square in the nuts. He grabbed his sack with both hands and folded like an accordion as he dropped to his knees, hard. So hard, in fact, I heard his kneecaps crack on the concrete.

Unfortunately, I'd misjudged which of the two was the mage.

Baldy was making complicated gestures with his hands and muttering in a language that might've been ancient Sumerian or gibberish for all I knew. I could care less; what I was mostly concerned about was the ball of fire coalescing between his hands.

"Aw, hell. Just remember, you asked for this," I said, raising my voice. I shot my hand out toward his eyes with my fingers extended in a classic bil jee strike. The bil jee, or finger jab, was one of Bruce Lee's favorites—both for its simplicity and its effectiveness.

The strike landed home, and I felt my fingertips sink into the squishy orb of his right eyeball. One thing most mages forgot was that it took time to cast a spell. Circle mages were used to having their hunter sidekicks closing the gap with their enemies, acting as a sort of human shield to give the mages time to spin up their magic. In this proximity, he'd have been better off throwing a punch.

Live and learn, I supposed. The mage stopped casting his spell immediately, and the fire dissipated as he reflexively lifted his hands to protect his eyes. Sadly for him, the spell hadn't completely dispersed, and he singed his eyebrows and eyelashes in the process.

"It's burning my eyes!" he screamed, batting at his face with his still flaming hands.

I couldn't imagine what burning your eyeballs felt like, but it had to hurt.

"Don't worry, man, I got this," I said as I popped the cap off my frozen mochaccino and tossed it in his face. Then I kicked him square in the nuts, harder than I'd kicked his partner. He collapsed to the ground, curled up in the fetal position.

I stepped over him on the way to my scooter. "There's your mochaccino, asshole. Now, tell all your buddies that I just want to be left the fuck alone. The next time you jackasses try to shake me down, I won't go this easy on you."

14

I knew I needed to move fast if I was going to catch Cécile at her hideout. Before the night was out, someone would find Cade. Or, his arms and legs would heal and he'd bust himself out of those restraints. Either way, the clock was ticking. I headed to the location where he'd said Cécile hid out during the day, parking a few blocks away from the witch's pad.

And what a pad it was—a condo on the upper floors of one of the ritzier high-rises downtown. To me, it was just another concrete monstrosity fucking up the view of the capitol building, but to others, living in such a building meant luxury and prestige. Condos in downtown high-rises went for a pretty penny; apparently, selling illusion charms and glamours to the city's supernatural underworld paid well. Or, she'd killed someone and stolen their identity. The more I thought about it, the more the latter option made sense.

A soucouyant fed in much the same way your typical vampire did, with a few major differences. First, they rarely killed their victims in one feeding, preferring instead to feed from the same person, over and over. And when soucouyants did kill their victims, they had the ability to steal their skin and assume their form.

Second, they preferred to shed their skin to travel and feed. In their non-corporeal form, they looked and moved like will-o'-the-wisps. In that form, they could travel great distances very quickly, slip in and out of homes unnoticed, and were very hard to kill. Unless you found their original skin sack, that was. Destroy that, and you destroyed the soucouyant, for good.

I hoped Cécile would be gone when I arrived. If so, I could take her skin sack, hide it, and use it as a bargaining chip to force her into helping me find the vampire. Of course, now that I knew what she was, I'd have to kill her before I went after my mystery vamp. No way I was going to leave yet another rogue vampire loose in the city. If I was lucky, Luther would bump my pay for killing Cécile, too.

It was close to four in the morning by the time I got to her floor. I'd had to take the stairs, since the lobby was guarded by security and the elevators only operated with keycards. By the time I hit the fourteenth floor, I felt like I was about to pass out. I swore I'd never let myself get out of shape again.

I knew she had to feed each night, because that's how soucouyants powered their magic. So, Cécile was likely to be elsewhere when I arrived. She'd have to be back before dawn, just like any other vampiric creature, so I needed to work fast. I disabled the wards on the door, spelled the locks open, and entered the apartment.

So this is how the other half lives, I thought as I carefully shut the door and listened for any sign of movement in the condo. All was silent. I made my way through the place, silver-inlaid sword in one hand and pistol in the other.

After clearing the living area and kitchen—and taking a moment to admire the million-dollar view of Ladybird Lake—I headed for the bedrooms. In the first, I found photos of a woman who looked like Cécile. At least, what her disguise had looked like at The Hammer and Anvil.

I searched the rest of the room, taking note of the woman's photos as I did. In every photo, she was smiling as she posed with what must have been her friends and family. Had Cécile been wearing that woman's skin earlier? I had no idea how the mechanics of the magic worked, but it was highly possible. That meant she'd killed the condo's occupant, just as I'd suspected.

Yeah, she was definitely going down.

The rest of the room was more or less your typical thirty-ish professional's bedroom. A large wardrobe in the closet. Historical romance and business books on the nightstand. A vibrator hidden in a lacquered jewelry box in the bottom drawer, along with a .38 pistol that she'd likely never had a chance to use against the witch. I felt like a voyeur as I searched what had once been this woman's private domain. But now was not the time to respect the privacy of the dead. I had to find the soucouyant's skin, and fast.

I continued tossing the place and found absolutely zip.

As I walked into the next bedroom, I smelled something familiar that stopped me in my tracks. It was a combination of desiccated flesh, grave dirt, and heme.

A vampire's lair.

The bed had been tossed aside, almost casually, and left tipped awkwardly against the wall. There were no windows in this space, which made it the perfect place for a vamp to rest during daylight hours. A large wooden box sat in the center of the room, roughly the size of a coffin. It looked to be a shipping crate of some sort. I snuck up to it and gently lifted the lid back.

Moist dirt covered the bottom, but it was otherwise empty.

Was this where the witch rested at night? Or could this have been where Raffy had been hiding out all along? And if so, were he and Cécile allies of convenience, or something more? Was he her maker? I'd never heard of a higher vampire making a different kind of vamp than their own kind—but with older vampires, anything was possible. Some delved into black magic, and I'd heard rumors of very old vamps summoning various kinds of supernatural creatures to serve them.

This case was getting crazier by the minute. I checked my watch; it'd be daylight soon. I needed to find that witch's skin and get the hell out of Dodge. Where had I not checked yet?

I had a flash of intuition and headed for the kitchen. I popped open the fridge, and sure enough, there sat a large stone mortar. I looked inside and found two neatly folded sets of human skin, with the hair and nails completely intact. I shuddered as I unfolded one to make sure it was what I'd been looking for. No doubt about it; it was the genuine article.

I stuffed the mortar into a shopping tote, tied it off with some string, and threw it in my Craneskin Bag. Then I scratched out a quick note on a nearby notepad, tore it off, and left it in the fridge. Once that was done, I beat feet out of there, heading for the stairwell just as fast as my long, lanky legs could carry me.

Somewhere around the fifth floor, I heard a high keening sound coming from somewhere above me. The witch's wailing cry echoed off the walls of the stairwell, filled with rage and grief. I ran faster, nearly stumbling as I hit the last set of stairs. I skidded out the stairwell door, around the corner, and ran for the front doors of the building at a sprint.

As I cleared the doors, the first rays of sunlight were beginning to peek over the horizon. I ran for the nearest open space, which was in the direction of Ladybird Lake. As I looked east to the sunrise, I noticed the last few bats flying for safety and darkness under the Congress Avenue Bridge. I suppressed a shiver as I spent a moment basking in the morning sun.

Safe, for now.

I headed back to the junkyard to prepare for nightfall, and to get some rest. Come sundown, things were going to get hairy. And I had a feeling it was going to be a long night.

15

A s I went home to prepare, I wondered if I should have stayed at the condo and attacked during daylight. It would have been a risky proposition, but one with a potential payoff as well. Vampires were weaker during the day, and exposure to sunlight was their one universal Achilles' heel. Problem was, that back bedroom would have been dark as night, even in the daytime. And if I'd ended up facing Cécile and Raffy at the same time, I'd have been toast for sure.

In her incorporeal form, Cécile would be a handful all by her lonesome. Wisps were hard enough to fight, because they moved fast, never tired, and only certain weapons had any effect on them. Add in the potential for magical attacks, and one of those little balls of light could do some serious damage. A soucouyant in wisp form had all the same advantages—plus they could feed on you, just as any vampire could in physical form.

So, fighting Cécile and a centuries-old vampire all at once was out of the question. Not a chance I'd risk it, even if it meant catching two vamps in their lair during daylight hours when they were weakest. No, my best shot was in keeping them separate by drawing Cécile out and then using her to lead me to Raffy.

To do that, my plan was simple. I'd drop the undead ward on the front gate of the junkyard, but leave the rest of the wards in place. That'd allow Cécile to enter the parking lot, but she wouldn't get much farther than that. Then we'd have a little chat, I'd get the info I needed—and afterward, I'd incinerate her skin sacks and end her worthless un-life for good.

I readied a few minor spells, rearranged my Craneskin Bag so I had the stuff I needed near at hand, then did some work around the yard before catching a few hours of sleep. At five o'clock, my alarm went off. I got up and had some coffee and a bowl of microwave ramen, then went to work.

The first task at hand was making sure no one was working late in the yard, shop, or warehouse. All I needed was for one of the other yard hands or a mechanic to decide to work late and become a snack for Cécile. I checked all the buildings and walked the yard; not a single soul was around, including Finnegas.

He was probably passed out somewhere in a gutter with a needle stuck in his arm. I'd long since stopped trying to rescue him, and had decided to leave him to suffer the consequences of his actions. At least it meant I wouldn't have to worry about him tonight. While he may have been two thousand years old, and once a powerful magic-user, I doubted he'd be worth two shits in a fight these days. Addiction was an unforgiving bitch, that was for sure.

It was getting close to dark. The note I'd left for Cécile told her to come to the junkyard after dark if she wanted her skin back. It was really no secret where I lived—everyone who was clued in around these parts knew that. It's just that no supernatural creature was stupid enough to try to accost me here. A few had tried and paid with their lives by tripping my wards. I might have been shit with most spells, but I knew how to set a ward like no one's business.

Plus, with all the metal around the yard, it made it damned uncomfortable for fae to come near. That part was an added bonus to living in a junkyard. The only bonus, really, besides the dirt-cheap rent.

I walked the yard one last time and checked my watch. It'd be sundown in fifteen minutes. I rattled the gates, making sure they were locked up tight. Then I dropped the ward that kept the undead out and took a seat on the front steps of the warehouse to wait.

It wasn't long after sundown when she arrived. Shortly after the eastern sky began to darken into night, I saw a ghostly ball of flame hurtling out of the sky toward the front gate of the yard. That was the only safe entry point for her kind at the moment, so over the gates she came. I sat on the steps and observed her as she approached, a sphere of pale orange and yellow flames that held the barest outline of a hag's face in the center.

When the sphere floated within ten feet of me, I held up a hand. "That's close enough, Cécile. Come any farther, and I'll start throwing handfuls of rice on the ground. You'll be counting grains until sunup—and then neither of us will get what we want."

The ball of swamp gas halted its advance, and the face within the fire became clearer and more distinct. The sphere grew brighter, save for the old hag's eyes. Those were two empty orbs, black as night and devoid of any light at all.

Her voice sounded like a roaring furnace as she spoke. "I should burn you to ash where you stand. Fry you to a crisp, and take what's mine."

In this form, she had just the slightest hint of a Creole accent that I hadn't noticed when she was in human form. It made me wonder how and when she'd been made. For all I knew, Cécile could be a few centuries old. Legend had it that when the French had colonized the Caribbean, European vampires fed on and infected their slaves. Some of these slaves had practiced black magic, and from that mix of magic, the first soucouyant had been born.

If she was that old, I needed to play this situation very carefully. She might have other tricks up her sleeve that made her far deadlier than I had originally anticipated.

I nodded and frowned. "Yes, you could do that. But then you'd never get what you came for—you can be sure of that."

The face in the flames appeared to sniff the air. "Where is it? My skin. I sense it is nowhere near. You playing games with me, boy?"

"It's very close by—but somewhere you could never find it, not in a million years." This was partially true, because whatever I put in my Craneskin Bag became dimensionally displaced. While her mortar and skins were within arm's reach, they were also in a completely different plane of existence, one she could never access. The Bag was attuned to me and me alone. I could have locked her mortar up in a bank vault and it wouldn't have been as secure.

"Tell me what you want."

I tsked. "Come now, Cécile—you know what I want. Tell me where to find the vampire called 'Raffy,' and I'll return your mortar and skin to you."

The face in the ball of flame laughed. "He'll kill you, just as easily as swatting a fly."

I made a show of examining my fingernails. "We tangled once, and he didn't get the better of me then. What makes you think he will the second time around?"

"Because he was toying with you. He wanted you to know what he was, so when he killed the woman you'd know you tried and failed to stop him."

I knew she was right, but I didn't care to let her see that. "Interesting. Well, your master may be old, but he's not invincible."

She bristled. "I have no master—not for a very long time. Rafael is my *maker*, but I do not serve at his command."

"Then tell me where I can find him, so we can conclude our business transaction."

She floated there, quiet for several seconds. "Fine, but know that you go to your death. Look for him where the night creatures rest. He'll be among his little brothers and sisters, hiding from the sunlight."

It took me a moment to puzzle out what she meant. "The bridge? You mean he doesn't stay at the condo with you?"

"Two old ones of our kind, living under the same roof? His years might dwarf mine, but he respects my sovereignty—as he has from the day he freed me. No, he would not trespass in my home, nor stoop so low as to impose on me in any way. That is why I still serve him."

Huh. "Cécile, one last question... why does a centuries-old vampire need to hide behind a glamour?"

She chuckled, and it sounded like cinders crackling in a campfire. "Seek him, and you will find out. Now, I have given you what you asked for. It is your turn now to give me what is mine."

"So it is." I reached into my bag and grabbed the mortar, rolling it across the parking lot so it landed beneath her. It was still wrapped inside the shopping tote I'd tucked it in earlier. But that didn't mean I hadn't messed with it since.

The soucouyant descended on the thing immediately, flaring with light as she burned the canvas shopping bag away from its contents. She spoke something in Creole, and one of the bundles of skin, hair, and nails floated out of the stone bowl. It unfolded itself and expanded to take the shape of an old hag. As it did, the fireball that was Cécile's incorporeal form collapsed in on itself, until it was just a tiny flicker of flame. Then, it flew into the skin sack's empty eye socket.

I watched as the flame expanded inside the skin sack, and plugged my ears as a short, sharp wail came from those dead, leathery lips.

"No, what have you dooonnn..."

Whoosh! The skin sack burst into flame and was immolated instantly, cutting off the witch's cry. The resulting flash was so hot that I cringed away and covered my face with my arms. An instant later, nothing remained but ash.

I walked over to the mortar and lit a match, carefully tossing it into the bowl on top of the second skin sack—the one that belonged to the poor woman who'd owned the condo. It took a few seconds, but then it too burst into flames along with the gunpowder, magnesium shavings, and sawdust I'd dumped inside each sack of skin. I'd only hoped that Cécile's wisp form would ignite it, but hadn't been sure it would work.

Luckily, my plan had gone off without a hitch. That was, until a seven-foot tall berserker werebear jumped over the gate and landed in the junkyard parking lot.

16

"Oh, you have got to be fucking kidding me," I muttered. I had the yard warded against all manner of supernatural creatures, but warding against 'thropes was tricky. They were the most human of all monsters, but they came in many different shapes, sizes, and species.

To ward against them, I'd had to create a separate spell for each type of 'thrope who might try to invade my home. I'd warded the place against werewolves, werecats, nāgas, lizard men, draconian shifters, and yes, even werebears. Finnegas had told me there was an easier way to do it, but he'd been too stoned to show me. So, I'd gone about it the hard way and tried to be as thorough as possible.

But from the looks of it, Cade's magic wasn't covered by my wards.

I guess berserkers really are a breed apart from werebears. Who knew?

Despite the apparent differences in how his magic worked, Cade Valison's shifted form looked just like any other werebear I'd seen. He was massively built—a good foot taller than me, and twice as broad. He was covered in fur from head to toe, with an elongated snout like a bear's and a mouth filled with sharp, nasty-looking teeth. But his limbs all articulated the same way a human's did, and he had paw-like hands with opposable thumbs.

Strangest of all, though, was the fact that he was wearing the same lamellar armor I'd seen him in earlier, along with loose woolen pants and a wide leather belt. I'd never seen a 'thrope in clothes before. He also had his hammer in one hand and a buckler in the other.

A shifter who wore armor and used magical weapons. *Peachy*. There was no way I was going to go toe-to-toe with this guy. Chances were good he'd get a lucky shot in with that hammer, beat me to a pulp, and then my other side would come out.

And that'd be bad news for everyone.

I needed to improvise.

He looked quite a bit fatter in this form—which was a very bear-like quality, I supposed. "So, Cade, fancy seeing you here. Did you just decide to stop by for dinner? Because, dude, from the looks of it, you really need to lay off the beer and pizza."

His gravelly voice bellowed at me from across the parking lot as he approached. "You should never have killed the witch. Now that she's dead, I am released from her magic." He flexed his paw-hands and his upper lip curled into a snarl. "And now I will have my revenge!"

"Seriously, man? 'Now I will have my revenge?' You've been watching too many Saturday morning cartoons." I did a little jig with my elbows out to the sides and imitated his voice. "Arrghh! I will have my revenge! Then Skeletor will give me a seat at the council table once more! Arrghh!"

Cade roared, and even from several yards away I could smell his breath. It reeked like raw meat and rotten strawberries, which was weird. But I supposed that if I'd been a berserker werebear, I'd have gone Paleo too.

"Mock me if you must, mortal. It'll only make your defeat that much sweeter."

I rolled my eyes. I needed this guy to chase me if I was going to put my plan into action. How hard could it be to get a berserker angry?

"Oh, just shut up and go berserk already. Or are you chicken?" I made chicken noises and flapped my elbows at my sides, strutting and pecking like a rooster.

"I... am... not... craven!" he roared.

Yep, that did it. Cade charged me, somehow bounding on all fours while still hanging onto his hammer. And all those stories you hear about how deceptively fast bears are, and how you can't outrun them so don't even try? Yeah, that was all pretty much true. I barely dove out of the way as he came at me, and caught a swipe of his claws across my back for my troubles.

I rolled up into a crouch and burst into a sprint, heading for the stacks of junk cars in the yard. I hoped I could lose him there, and then draw him into a trap. As I fled, warm, sticky blood ran from the wounds on my upper back. I tested my range of motion on the move, and while the wounds bled freely, they appeared to be superficial.

I glanced back to see where Cade was and wished I hadn't. Due to his bulk, he wasn't the most graceful creature—but he was hellaciously quick in the straightaway.

So, I took every twist, turn, and corner I could to lose him in the maze that was my uncle's junkyard. Where I could make hairpin turns and switch direction quickly, Cade slid around corners, crashing into old cars and piles of junk. The more I evaded him, the angrier he got.

I rounded one last corner and sprinted toward a fifteen-foot wall of cars just ahead. I looked for an opening in the wall and spotted a window in the cab of a sedan that wasn't completely flattened. The car had once been someone's track toy, and it still had a roll cage welded into the cab.

Perfect.

I dove through the window. Thankfully, the rest of the interior had been stripped down to bare metal to reduce weight and for safety reasons. That left plenty of room for me to climb through. I scrambled out the other side, just as Cade crashed into the door.

I paused for a second as I scrambled free, just to make sure the berserker couldn't fit through the narrow gap. He couldn't, but he was doing his damnedest and the stack was swaying like crazy. I decided to avoid getting crushed and took off toward my goal, knowing I'd only have a minute or so to prepare before Cade found a way around.

A few seconds later, I turned the corner around the stacks and saw what I needed. The crusher and crane. I climbed into the crane's cab, firing it up and positioning a junked, stripped car several yards above the crusher. I cast a quick spell on the controls, hoping I got it right. Otherwise, my plan would fail and I'd be screwed.

I jumped out of the crane's cab and ran to the baler crusher, firing it up so the hydraulics would be primed and ready to go. The baler crusher was the coolest piece of equipment in the yard. It could flatten a minivan and then crush it into a twenty-four-inch cube in under two minutes. And once the lid dropped on that bad boy, one hundred and fifty tons of downward force ensured that nothing was getting out of that thing.

Once I had everything in place, I stood atop the baler and waited. And waited. And waited. Finally, I realized that Cade had gotten lost in the yard. In fact, I could hear him roaring and crashing into things in the distance. I resorted to calling for him, yelling taunts and insults every few seconds to allow him to home in on my voice.

A minute or so later, the fool came barreling into the crushing area of the yard. I stood balanced on top of the crusher, right on the far edge as I yelled at him one last time.

"Finally found me? Took you long enough. Alright, Smokey, let's end this. Come at me, bro!"

Sure enough, he took the bait. The berserker may have been strong and fast, but lucky for me he was also blinded by rage. He raced across the yard toward me, accelerating with every bounding step.

This was going to be close.

Just as I expected, he neared the crusher and took a running leap at me, intending to either tackle me off the edge or hammer me into a pulp. I wasn't sure which, and I didn't care. As soon as he was airborne I triggered my spell, releasing the crane and the stripped down car chassis it held suspended over the crusher.

But I was just a tad too slow in triggering the spell. While the car caught Cade as it fell, it only caught the back half of him. He gave me a glancing blow to the chest with his hammer as the car crushed his legs. I fell off the crusher with the wind knocked out of me, feeling like Cade had broken a rib or two. I landed in the dirt of the yard, flat on my back, trying to work air back into my lungs. I felt as though I had a car crushing me as well.

I laid there, stunned, until I felt a breeze caress my face. A woman's voice filled my ear.

C'mon, Colin. Get up. Get up!

Jesse's voice. I began to stir as a roar came from inside the crusher.

I heard metal shifting and scraping upon itself. A clawed, furred hand appeared on the edge of the crusher wall. The berserker may have been badly injured, but he was pulling himself free. Now that his shifter magic wasn't being suppressed, he'd heal quickly—and I'd have no way to stop him.

I rolled over and came up on my knees, coughing and wheezing as I pulled air into my chest one mouthful at a time. I half-stumbled and half-crawled to the controls, and hit the switch just as Cade's other arm popped over the side of the crusher, holding his hammer.

The lid dropped on the contents of the baler, slicing the berserker's left hand off at the wrist, and his right arm at the elbow. Both fell to the ground next to the crusher, along with the Norseman's war hammer.

There was another, muffled roar from inside the crusher, followed by a scream. As the lid dropped farther and the machinery did its work, the screams died away. Soon, all I could hear were the sounds of hydraulics, two tons of metal, and a berserker being crushed into a two-foot cube.

I laid on the ground, staring up at the night sky. I wondered what I was going to do with the parts that hadn't been pulverized in the machine.

A pale, dirty, bearded face appeared above me. "Good thinking, using the machinery like that. That berserker would've torn you to pieces, for sure. Didn't think you still had it in you."

I felt my chest and ribcage to see if I had any broken ribs. I didn't, but I was going to be hurting in the morning. I sat up and leaned against the crusher, taking a moment before I answered. Finnegas was dressed in an old pair of gray sweats, a wife beater, and not much else. He swayed back and forth in the moonlight and took a swig from a liquor bottle as he watched me wheeze and bleed.

"Good to see you too, old man. Were you watching the whole time?"

"Not until the damned thing crashed into the car I was sleeping in and woke me up."

I rubbed my chest and sighed. "And it didn't occur to you that I might have needed an assist?"

He belched and scratched his belly with grubby fingernails. "Nah, you seemed to have it under control." Finnegas looked at the severed limbs on the ground. "Tell you what—if you can spare a few bucks, I'll help you clean this whole mess up. It'll be like it never happened."

I let my head drop back to rest against the crusher and closed my eyes. "You'll do it anyway, because you owe me, Finn. Then I'll buy you some breakfast and a couple cartons of smokes." I cracked open an eye to gauge his response. "Deal?"

His face was a mask of pain, disguised by a scowl. The old man hung his head and nodded slowly. "You're right, I do owe you. Let's get this place cleaned up."

He offered me a hand and I took it, staggering to my feet with his help.

"And, Finn?"

"What?"

"You're not pawning the hammer."

17

I awoke late the next morning, well after the yard had opened for business. Finnegas, true to his word, had somehow cleaned up all signs of the previous night's battles. He'd also helped me dress my wounds. Even after several hours of rest, I felt like I'd wrestled a bear—and lost. Which may as well have been the case.

I rolled over and sat up, wincing at the pain in my ribs. My phone blinked with unread messages.

-Heard you now have a lead on our elusive friend. L wishes to speak to you immediately.-

Guess that meant I was headed to the coffee shop this morning. I figured if Luther wanted to see me "immediately," it meant he'd be there. Some older vamps didn't have to sleep during the day. Luther was known to be a daytime vamp, and was usually at his place of business pulling espressos for customers until noon or so. Then he'd take a break—a vampire had to keep up appearances—and be back at it after sundown.

I threw on a pair of jeans, moving gingerly. Bruised ribs sucked, but it was a common injury, so I was used to it. I slapped some arnica tonic and Chinese *dit da jow* liniment on the areas I could reach. Then I wrapped my chest with an ACE bandage and headed out the door.

When I got to the coffee shop, I made sure to case the place before I headed inside. Now that I'd screwed with two Circle teams, chances were good they'd be looking for revenge. Sooner made more sense than later, but you never could tell with those jackasses. The coast was clear, so I hopped off my scooter and snuck in the back entrance.

Luther spotted me right away as I walked in. He gave me a quick look of acknowledgment before tending to the customers in line. As he was filling orders, he slapped a frozen mochaccino and a couple of croissants on the counter and called out my name.

"On the house," he said with a wink. Yeah, Luther was turning out to be alright.

I headed to a table in the back and sat down, and spent the next several minutes enjoying the free grub and coffee while I did some people-watching. It amused me to no end that the humans who came in had no idea they were standing just a few feet away from an apex predator—and one that other predators feared. It was kind of like watching a group of tourists walk by the lion's cage at the zoo, none of them knowing that the door to the cage was open, just out of their line of sight.

One of the baristas took over for the vamp, and instead of calling me back to his office, he sat down at my table.

"How do you like the coffee?" he asked.

"It's good. Hell of a lot better than Mickey D's, that's for sure."

He smiled without showing much teeth—most vamps only showed their teeth when they meant to scare someone, or kill them—and leaned an elbow on the table.

"I made it with my special cold brew. No bitterness to the coffee that way, so you don't have to sweeten the drink as much.

Makes for a lot smoother experience, and you can still detect the flavor notes, even in a cold beverage."

I held the cup up and examined it. "I'm honestly not that much of a connoisseur, but I can tell you that it's damned good coffee."

He chuckled. "Hang around here long enough, and you'll learn. Now, regarding that old friend of ours. Did you find out where he was staying?"

"Downtown. That's if the information was correct."

"Hmm. Yes, I heard there were complications. We agreed on just one, so adjustments will need to be made at week's end."

I took that to mean I'd be getting paid a bonus for taking out the soucouyant. It almost made the busted ribs worth it.

"Luther, there's one thing you should know." He studied me without twitching an eyelash. "This... old friend. He looks quite young for his age. Astonishingly so, if I'm not mistaken."

"I see." Luther stared out the window, as if contemplating a difficult problem. Or maybe, he was speaking to another vampire telepathically—who knew? "Then I will accompany you on your visit. This will not affect the terms of our original arrangement, of course."

He stood abruptly. "Meet me at the Vaughan statue two hours before sunrise." He turned on his heel and headed toward the counter, but paused mid-step to address me over his shoulder. "I know I probably don't need to say this, but dress to impress."

I figured that meant I should come in my full battle-rattle. I nodded, then turned my attention back to my drink and the last few morsels of croissant on my plate. Just as I was finishing up, a perky five-foot-nothing Hispanic girl with a devilish gleam in her eye plopped down across from me.

Belladonna leaned in and snagged my drink away from me,

taking the last few sips and setting it down. She licked her lips and smiled demurely.

"Heya, loverboy. Miss me?"

"Hi, Bells. Honestly, you're a bit hard to miss in that outfit."

Belladonna always dressed to kill, literally and figuratively. Today's outfit consisted of knee boots over skintight jeans that were missing a few inches of material along the side seams. In place of that material, they'd been laced up with some sort of leather string, like a corset.

Over that, she wore an oversized Joan Jett concert t-shirt that had been artfully sliced, tied, and otherwise rearranged so it showed more skin that it covered. Underneath, a black and red lace bra peeked out. A black leather biker jacket made the whole getup a lot less scandalous, serving double-duty in concealing the arsenal of weapons she always carried.

She sat up straighter, reaching out to run a finger down the back of my hand. "Why, Colin, thank you. I do believe that's the nicest thing you've ever said to me."

I shrugged. "Just stating facts. What brings you looking for me this morning?"

She leaned away from me in her chair, throwing an arm over its back as she crossed her legs. The whole pose looked damned uncomfortable to me, but somehow she made it look casual.

"Who says I came looking for you? Maybe I was just here to grab some coffee and happened to see you sitting by your lonesome."

"One, because you're never up this early. And two, because you look like the cat who ate the canary. You going to tell me what's up, or not?"

"I can never fool you, Colin. And I really don't have to, do I? That's what I've always liked about you." She uncrossed her legs and leaned in. "Rumor has it you made Jackson and Collins look like a couple of fools. Rumor also has it there's a bounty pool running, with the kitty going to the first team that teaches you a lesson."

"Yeah? And how does your partner feel about that?"

"Oh, he hates your guts. I think he kicked in a double-share, just for the hell of it."

I smiled. "Or maybe because his partner refused to participate."

"Maybe. But he still hates your guts."

"The feeling is mutual. You can tell him I said so."

"I will. It'll drive him nuts that I ran into you." Bells was kind of sort of dating her partner, Crowley. Unofficially, of course. What she saw in the guy was beyond me, but for now it was keeping her from making the full court press on me. I wasn't quite ready for a relationship yet, so I wasn't complaining.

She stood, placing her hands on the table and leaning over me, uncomfortably close as she whispered in my ear. "There's also some chatter about a missing werebear and witch. You wouldn't happen to know anything about that, would you?"

Man, news traveled fast. The last thing I wanted was to be pegged for killing Cade, because I did not need a vengeful deity hunting my ass. No way was I fessing up to that mess.

"Nope, not a thing. First I've heard of it."

Her lips brushed my cheek as she stood, and I suppressed an involuntary shiver. I'd be suppressing other things as well if she did that again.

"Well, that's good, I suppose. But you would tell me if you got back in the game again, right?"

"I would, most definitely."

She slapped me playfully on the cheek—once, twice.

"Liar."

I watched her leave and sighed. Heartbroken or not, I had to admit the girl knew how to get a guy's motor running. I shook it off, then set my mind on planning for the night's events.

18

S tevie Ray Vaughan was a local legend here in the state capital, and even though he'd actually been from Dallas, he'd made his bones on the Austin music scene. That made him an adopted son of the city, which was why locals had decided to memorialize his life and passing in art. As perhaps the finest modern blues guitarist of his time, he certainly deserved the recognition.

Unfortunately, the bronze statue that had been commissioned to memorialize him was ugly as all hell. In my opinion, it failed to capture the energy and enthusiasm that SRV had displayed in every musical performance. But since it had become a popular tourist stop and a beloved city landmark, the chances that he'd get a statue that more accurately depicted his likeness were slim to none.

I sighed as I walked past it, because the man deserved better.

I'd already decided to wait for Luther from a concealed place nearby. The memorial was located along a popular hike and bike trail at Auditorium Shores, or whatever the hell they were calling it now. Even at this late hour—or early hour, depending on how you looked at it—there was traffic on the pathways.

I'd tucked all my gear away and out of sight inside my Crane-skin Bag, but I wore a complete set of motorcycle leathers and steel-toed combat boots. The getup didn't exactly allow me to blend into my environment, so I headed off the trail to a stand of trees nearby.

"You don't care for the statue?"

Luther's voice came from behind, startling me. I'd already cast a night vision cantrip and made sure I was alone before settling in to wait. There wasn't much cover here, only a lot of shadow, and he hadn't made a single sound to tip me off to his arrival. To say I was surprised that he'd snuck up on me would have been an understatement.

I played it off, even though I knew he'd seen me jump. "I get what the artist was trying to do. But I think he should have reversed the images. The statue should be rocking out, and the shadow should be in repose. But then again, what do I know about art?"

The vamp walked up beside me and gazed across the lawn at the statue. "I knew him. He was a good man, after he got sober. Really loved his fans."

I glanced at Luther out of the corner of my eye. "You a blues fan?"

He smiled. "From the very beginning." In an instant, his expression and voice grew hard and serious. "Now, tell me about this vampire who has the audacity to hunt in my city."

"Goes by the name of Rafael. The witch I killed claimed that he was her maker. Also insinuated that he was older than sex. And I believe she provided him with a glamour to conceal his appearance."

"Interesting. And his lair?"

I pointed downriver, along the shoreline toward the east. "She said I'd find him 'where the night creatures took shelter,' or something to that effect. The only thing that came to mind was the bat colony under the Congress Avenue Bridge."

"If he can take the form of a bat, then he must be old." Luther stroked his chin as he contemplated the information. "Our primary challenge will be to conclude this situation without drawing public attention. There's a hotel on the south shore between First Street and Congress. I'll issue a challenge to Rafael and draw him to that location. You will go to the roof and remain hidden until my signal, at which time you will join the battle."

"I can do that. What's the plan?"

"If this vampire is as old as I think he is, my natural weapons will not be enough to kill him. Silver and fire will be required. I can wield neither without risking damage to myself, which is where you come in. He'll likely outmatch me in every category but speed. There, I should have the advantage. Once I get him on the defensive, come in and help me finish the job."

"Sounds simple enough. Give me fifteen minutes to get to the rooftop."

"You'll need to be there in ten. Be ready." With that, Luther walked off into the shadows. His retreating form melted into the night and dissipated like mist. And like that, he was just *gone*.

"So that's how he snuck up on me," I muttered as I headed off at a jog for the hotel Luther had referenced. "I *really* need to get better at using magic."

Sneaking into the hotel was a piece of cake, and getting up to the roof was simply a matter of magically picking the lock on the roof access door. I spent a minute scoping the place out and then hid under an old tarp behind some HVAC equipment, making sure I had a clear view of most of the roof.

Moments later, Luther walked out of the shadows and strolled to the center of the rooftop. One moment he wasn't there, and the next he was. Whether he was transforming into mist and floating from place to place, using illusory magic and vampire speed to conceal himself, or teleporting from shadow to shadow, I couldn't tell. What I did know was that it was damned impressive, and it made me wonder what tricks Rafael might also have up his sleeve.

Luther stood in the open, arms crossed and waiting. No more than a minute later, a swarm of bats flew down from the night sky. Right before my eyes, they coalesced into the shape of a man. A heartbeat later, they transformed from a dark cluster of wings and fur into a flesh and blood person.

Rafael.

I'm a little out of my depth, I thought. *Maybe more than a little.*

I checked to make sure my weapons were close at hand. I had my pistol holstered on my hip, loaded with silver-tipped bullets and tracers. I had a shoulder harness filled with silver blades and spikes. I had my silver-inlaid short sword at my hip, and a crossbow loaded with a silver-tipped bolt at my feet. And I had a couple of homemade napalm bombs in my bag—but because Luther was just as vulnerable to fire, they'd be a last resort. The only thing I didn't have was garlic and a cross. In my experience, neither had much effect on vamps, other than giving them a good laugh.

Satisfied that I was as ready as I could be, I settled in to eavesdrop and enjoy the show.

Luther and Rafael stared at each other across a distance of no more than twenty-five feet. For an older vampire, that was kissing distance. They were just that fast.

Rafael smiled, showing his teeth. Just as when I'd first met him, he was dressed to the nines in a sharp tailored suit, expensive Italian shoes, silk shirt, and a Rolex. Now that I knew it was all a façade, I wanted to see what was underneath the glamour. I shifted my vision to my second sight, focusing my will to see beyond the spell.

What I saw was revolting. Rafael was a nos-type vampire, a nosferatu. Typically, they were a more primitive sort of vamp. They were uglier, less intelligent, and more bestial than the higher species of their kind. While higher vampires almost always looked like pale, beautiful humans, nos-types looked like their namesake. They had grey, mottled skin, bat-like pointed ears, a skeletal build, and hands and feet that ended in razor-sharp claws.

Most striking of all, though, was their teeth. While higher vampires had elongated incisors, nosferatu had an entire mouthful of needle-sharp dentition. And while a higher vamp could feed on a human without causing lasting damage, a nos-type fed by savaging the chosen victim's flesh. Those bitten rarely survived.

I'd never known a nos to be all that powerful. The ones I'd hunted were more like vermin than apex predators. This Rafael was something different, something I'd never run into before. Old, dangerous, and crafty.

It made me wonder if confronting him like this was the right choice. I guess I could have just waited until daylight and tossed a couple of napalm bombs under the bridge. But that would have required hurting all those innocent bats in the colony. I didn't think I could barbecue several thousand bats just to get at one vampire.

Then I realized I could have used a giant parabolic mirror, to reflect sunlight up into the deep crevices under the bridge where the bats nested. Sure thing. I could have just run to the giant parabolic mirror store, set up a series of them in Rube Goldberg fashion, and fried the vamp for good.

Shit. Hindsight was always 20/20.

Too late for the MacGuyer solution now, Colin. Better be ready to rumble.

19

L uther spoke, bringing my attention back to the present.
"You are the one who calls himself Rafael?"

"I am. And you are Luther, master of the local coven, here to teach me a lesson for invading your dominion."

Luther stood statue-still as he replied. "If you wanted to kill indiscriminately, you should have gone to New Orleans. Unfortunately, you chose to kill in my city. We do not kill humans here."

Rafael tossed his head back and released a throaty laugh at the night sky. "Who has ever heard of vampires who do not hunt, who do not kill? We are the superior race. Humans are cattle for our kind. We kill because it pleases us, and so that we may survive. It has always been this way. To pretend otherwise is to deny our history and nature."

Luther barely twitched a muscle. "Be that as it may, the law here is that we do not kill humans."

Rafael's face darkened. "There is no such law among our kind."

"Among vampire-kind, I am the law here. And the penalty for breaking my law is death."

The nosferatu's expression softened to amusement again. "You may be elder to your coven members, but I am ancient. I have seen civilizations rise and fall. I have walked with pharaohs and watched as the Great Pyramids were built, back when the lands surrounding Giza were rich and verdant. I whispered in Nero's ear and laughed with him as Rome burned. I feasted during the Black Plague and roamed across the sea to the New World with Raleigh. I am the answer to the mystery of the Lost Colony. I am the lasting night... I am death."

I am the night? Really? Self-awareness, zero. Hubris, one. I stifled a laugh and shifted my weight to prevent my legs from going to sleep.

Luther gave a barely perceptible shrug. "Nevertheless, you have entered my dominion and ignored my authority. And I say again, the penalty for this is death."

"Pfah! I grow tired of this exchange." Rafael extended an arm toward Luther, beckoning him to approach. "Kill me then, if you can."

I didn't exactly catch what happened next, but it appeared as though Luther popped in and out of shadow, all around Rafael. There'd be a black puff of smoke, and then Luther's head and arm or upper torso would appear out of it. He'd strike, or slash, or bite—and then, poof. He'd disappear, only to reappear again a second later, in a different place to strike again from another angle.

Most of his attacks landed, but they seemed to have little effect. While each attack rocked Rafael, he appeared to be absorbing every strike without suffering much damage.

"Enough!" Rafael finally yelled, leaping a good forty feet into the air to get clear of Luther's barrage.

That's when the real Rafael showed up.

All pretense of his humanity fell away with the glamour in an instant. And as Rafael's true form was revealed, a further, unexpected transformation occurred. The nosferatu outstretched his arms, and they transformed into huge, hooked, bat-like wings. He grew larger at the same time, taking on extra mass in a manner that defied logic and physics. Although it was difficult to gauge his size accurately as he hovered in the air, I estimated that he'd gained between one and two feet in height.

"Well, so much for not drawing attention to ourselves," I muttered. Somehow, I doubted that a seven-foot tall man-bat with a twenty-five-foot wingspan would escape the notice of the local population. The only consolation was the fact that it was still dark outside, and there were few people out and about at this hour. Hopefully, any and all reports would be chalked up to mass hysteria.

So long as no one filmed it.

Luther blinked back into existence a few feet away from my hiding spot and whispered without moving his lips. I guessed when you were centuries old, you picked up a few hobbies, like ventriloquism.

"When we engage in battle again, choose your moment carefully. You will not get a second chance."

I whispered back. "Gotcha. I'll wait 'til the time is right, and banzai this motherfucker with everything I have on me." *No pressure there, or anything. Sheesh.*

Rafael the super-nosferatu chose that moment to swoop down at Luther, dive-bombing him like a peregrine falcon descending on a rabbit. Luther appeared to be caught in indecision as he watched the winged nos dropping toward him. Then, at the last moment, he zipped out of the way.

With a single beat of those massive wings, Rafael banked skyward again. I worked the math out in my head and determined it was impossible for those wings to lift his mass and move him that quickly through the air. There had to be some sort of telekinetic levitation and propulsion involved as well. He climbed into the sky and dove at Luther three more times. Each time, the coven leader "blinked" out of the way.

I noted two things of interest during those three attacks.

First, vampire magic was weird.

And second, Luther was tiring. Apparently, there were limits to his powers. I could only surmise that he powered up on blood and therefore had a finite supply of energy to fuel his vampire speed. If that was the case, I also assumed that he wasn't feeding as well or as often as Rafael. It had to be hard to feed without killing humans. Volunteers would be difficult to come by. They'd have to be rotated so they weren't bled into anemia, and feedings would have to be limited... rationed, even.

I realized then how much danger Luther faced. From the looks of it, Rafael would have him in a few more passes. All he'd have to do would be to grab Luther, take him up a few thousand feet, and let terminal velocity do the rest.

Shit.

I decided to make my move. I loosened my sword in my scabbard, picked up the crossbow, and grabbed the edge of the tarp. Timing would be everything. I watched and waited until Rafael hit peak altitude. He dropped, and I ran, leading him off as I fired the crossbow. I didn't even break stride as I dropped it, drawing my sword in one hand and my pistol in the other.

Just as I was drawing a bead on Rafael, the crossbow bolt pierced his wing. Where Luther's attacks had almost immediately healed or had no effect, the silver bolt tore a gaping hole in his wing that grew larger as the wind whipped through it. Rafael's graceful dive became a plummet, and I filled him with lead, silver, and burning magnesium on the way down—right before he crash-landed on the roof.

I closed the gap immediately, drawing back for a powerful overhead slash at his exposed neck.

And I was stopped dead in my tracks as one of those massive

wings lashed out, slapping me across my torso. I was flung across the rooftop, where I skidded to an abrupt stop against a vent pipe.

I shook it off just in time to look up and see a now wingless Rafael rocketing across the roof at me. I fired the last few rounds from my pistol at him and watched as they punched holes in his chest, legs, and face. He didn't seem to mind, and snatched me up in a massive clawed hand by the neck, lifting me off my feet and holding me up like a prize.

"Luther, you brought me a gift. This is the meddler who killed Cécile. Such a shame. It will take me some time to create another like her. I will derive much pleasure in bleeding this one dry."

I struggled against his grip, slashing at his arm with my sword as I kicked and fought. I stabbed my sword through his arm, eliciting a roar from the nos. He plucked the sword free and tossed it away, over the side of the building.

"That was my favorite sword, dick," I croaked as he held me suspended a foot off the ground.

He chuckled. "Such anger and defiance. Perhaps I should turn you, and make you my servant instead."

Luther's voice echoed from over my left shoulder. "I wouldn't do that if I were you. Moreover, I would advise you to set the boy down, and negotiate a truce."

"I'm... no... boy," I groaned, still kicking weakly in a vain effort to free myself.

The two old vamps ignored me.

Rafael turned his massive chiropteran head to acknowledge Luther. "What reason would I have to spare him? We've already established that neither of you can stop me."

I reached into my Bag as he spoke, grabbing one of the napalm bombs. Hell if I was going to become a vamp. I'd go out in a blaze of glory before that happened.

Suddenly, I felt Luther's hand like a vice on my wrist. "Colin, wait."

What the fuck, Luther?

Luther continued, addressing Rafael now. "I would not be the one to stop you. And Colin here wouldn't, either. At least, not *this* Colin. Look closer at the prey you hold in your hand, Rafael. Look deeper, and tell me what you see."

The nosferatu's eyes narrowed as he inspected me, then they widened. "It's not possible... this is a trick!"

Luther walked slowly into my line of sight to my left, hands clasped behind his back like a college professor on a leisurely stroll. "I assure you, this is no trick. Feed from him, and the thing inside him will be released. Try to turn him, and the same will happen. And as you and I well know, it will destroy you. Perhaps even the both of us."

Rafael turned me left and right, examining me like a slab of meat. After several seconds of being scrutinized by Max Shreck, he dropped me like a hot rock.

"You tell the truth. The god-giants return."

I sat there in a heap, rubbing my neck, while Luther regarded Rafael. He tilted his head slightly. "In a manner of speaking, yes. Things are changing, Rafael. Now you see why I choose to live in peace with humans. An alliance may very well be necessary for our survival in days to come."

Rafael grunted. "I could still kill you."

Luther nodded. "You could. But then this young man would hunt you to the ends of the earth. You would have no rest. He would either find you and destroy you during your time of rest or confront you and force you to trigger his ríastrad. Either way, you would be destroyed."

I shook my head in disbelief and chuckled despite the situation. All this time, Luther had known I couldn't beat Rafael. He'd also been well aware that he couldn't defeat him, either. So, he'd used me as his pawn. A pawn who could be crowned to destroy the king.

"Still here, you know," I muttered from the asphalt roof of the building.

Again, the two vampires ignored me. They stared at each other a good long while.

Finally, Rafael's shoulders slumped. "Tell me, master of the Austin vampire coven... what are your terms?"

EPILOGUE

The next day, I sat in Luther's office at the coffee shop. I sipped on a damned good cappuccino as he stared at me from across his desk.

"I regret that I couldn't let you in on my plan. However, I knew that ultimately you'd be in no grave danger. And, you are the only creature in Austin—save Maeve, perhaps—that he would fear."

I rubbed the bruises on my neck. I looked like I'd been making out with a Dyson vacuum. "Would've been nice if you'd got her to kick him out of town."

His forehead creased for a moment, then his expression went flat again. "I doubt that the Queen of the Austin fae has any interest in chasing vampires from her city. If she did, I would be gone by now. To her, one vampire is the same as another. We pose no threat to Maeve."

He tapped a pencil on the table, drumming the eraser like the world's fastest metronome. The pencil froze, and he pointed it at me. "However, after last night's events, she may begin to take an interest in you. Such a story will very likely intrigue her... and being the focus of her intrigue is not a circumstance I would wish on any mortal."

"Great."

He frowned. "Perhaps you'll escape her notice. I only mention it so you can be prepared. If you're ever called into her presence, be on your guard."

"I'll keep that in mind. Thanks for the warning."

The old vampire sat up straighter and smiled. "Now, to the business at hand. Your compensation."

He pushed a thick envelope across the desk to me. I peeked inside; it was what he'd promised and more. That would definitely help pay for my tuition. Then I thought about Charlene's kids.

Damn it.

I pushed the envelope back across the desk to him. "Is there any way you can get this to Charlene's family? You know, to help them out?"

Luther blinked—once, twice. "You mean the children of the last woman he killed." I nodded. "Consider it done. I'll have my attorneys set up a trust fund in each child's name. Also, I made some calls. The Circle won't be bothering you again."

"Thanks, Luther."

"Don't mention it. Colin, I owe you a great debt—beyond whatever recompense we first agreed upon. Don't be a stranger around here. I find your sense of honor to be... compelling." He paused, as if searching for the right words. "If you ever need anything, feel free to call on me and mine."

I took a sip of coffee and smirked. "Alright... just as long as you don't try to turn me metro."

Suddenly, the serious vampire coven master was gone, and the queen was back. Luther gave me snaps and an "oh no you didn't" look. "Pretty white boy, you might be cute, but believe me —you could use a little style advice from Luther."

I chuckled into my coffee. "I'll take that under advisement, based on the authority of the source."

He shook his head and cocked an ear. "Hmmm... perfect timing. Sounds like that hot little Spanish number is out there looking for you. Just for that remark, I'm going to let her know you're here."

"Luther, wait—"

And like that, he was gone. A few seconds later, I heard a knock at the office door.

"Loverboy, I know you're in there. Are you trying to avoid me?" More knocking. "I'm just going to keep knocking until you come out, you know."

I hung my head. "Thanks, Luther," I whispered.

Somewhere, from the front of the cafe, I swear I heard him laugh.

Ready for more Colin McCool? Click here to check out Junkyard Druid, the first full-length novel in the Colin McCool Paranormal Suspense and Urban Fantasy series!

Made in the USA
Monee, IL
18 March 2024

55209135R00066